Unmasked

Marie Tuhart

https://www.marietuhart.com/

QUALITY CONTROL: We strive to produce error-free books, but even with all the eyes that see the story during the production process, slips get by. So please, if you find a typo or any formatting issues, please let us know at marie@marietuhart.com so that we may correct it.

Thank you!

Unmasked

Wicked Sanctuary: Surrender your inhibitions.

They say opposites attract.

A woman who likes her life as it is, uncomplicated.

A dominant man who wants her.

Ellie Tanner loves her party planning business, and it has brought her to a new adventure. Wicked Sanctuary. She needs a place where she can forget everything and relax. But her mentor causes sparks to fly. He's a complication she doesn't need.

Logan Wolfe had never planned to be a mentor, but when Max asks him to take on Ellie, Logan jumps in feet first. The feisty woman has awakened the beast in him. Throw in her innocence, sass, and a very different Halloween party, and life gets very interesting.

Can they see past their issues to find their HEA?

ACKNOWLEGMENTS

There are several people I want to thank for supporting me through this book:

Laurie, thank you for all your support and writing sessions.

Red Quill Editing team, you are the best team to work with. You can always make me laugh. And you always, always make my writing better.

Publisher's Note: This book contains a dominant male, spunky heroine, sexy situations, violence around police work and trauma. No Artificial Intelligence was used in the crafting of this book.

To My Readers:

This book contains elements of the BDSM lifestyle that are only true to life in this book. There are various relationship dynamics in the lifestyle, which are decided between the people involved. While I have researched and talked with people in the lifestyle, this is my take on how my characters choose to live.

If you decide to explore the lifestyle yourself, please remember to always be safe. Never go home with someone you don't know. Attend a munch or a small get-together first to see if this is something you want in your life. Reading and living are very different.

FYI: Ellie was introduced in *Untamed.*

Enjoy.

Chapter 1

Ellie Tanner grinned as one of the male strippers pulled Sierra on stage. She'd been a little doubtful about having the bachelorette party at The Oasis, but all seemed to be going well. Max Preston, Sierra's fiancé and owner of the local BDSM club, apparently hadn't objected.

"Great party," Tessa, one of the bridesmaids, commented.

"I'm glad it's working out."

"We're loving it," Crystal said. She was the other bridesmaid. Both had contacted Ellie and asked her to have the party here. Ellie had done her due diligence and checked the place out, chatted with the owner, and made the decision it would be okay. Some might think she was going overboard, but she liked providing the best experience she could for her clients.

"Let's dance," one of the other women called out.

Sierra left the stage and joined the women on the dance floor. Ellie couldn't stop smiling as the music grew louder. She started cleaning up the table, throwing away the paper from the presents, penis shaped plates from the cake, kinky presents in bags, and other things.

All in all, this was successful party.

"Come on, Ellie." Regina tugged at her hand to get her out on the dance floor.

"Sorry. I'm the planner, not a guest." This was her standard line. She stood on the sidelines, watching the women. She didn't involve herself in her clients' lives any more than necessary, although, with Sierra, it was a little harder. In between meetings with her, Crystal, and Tessa about the bachelorette party, she'd also planned Sierra's wedding.

They'd had several get-togethers at Max and Sierra's home and at the club. Ellie had been curious about Wicked Sanctuary, and Sierra had been gracious enough to show her around and talk with her about the BDSM lifestyle.

Regina opened her mouth. "Oh shit."

"What?" Sierra yelled.

"Turn around," Regina said.

Ellie turned, following Regina's gaze.

"Shit is right," Sierra commented as her eyes grew wide.

"Wow," Ellie said under her breath. She could only stare at the line of men standing shoulder-to-shoulder with their arms crossed over their chests and staring at the group. The men were similarly dressed in jeans and t-shirts, their unwavering gazes on the women. Damn, they looked impressive.

Their testosterone and dominance filled the air. A shiver snaked up Ellie's spine. She recognized Max, Jordan, and Damon, but not the rest of the men, although she suspected they were attached to the other women still here at the party. But when she counted men, there was an extra.

He stood at the end, however, there was something about him that screamed, *I'm in charge*. His short dark hair gave off the *don't mess with me* vibe. He was tall with wide shoulders. Dressed much like the others in dark clothing, he looked… Ferocious wasn't the right word. He didn't look angry or upset, more intrigued than anything. Maybe it was the way he stood. Legs apart, arms crossed over chest. Just like the other men. No, it was more than that, because all the guys held the same stance. He only had eyes for her. That was the difference. That and the intensity of his gaze made Ellie's heart flutter. Those dark brown eyes never left her face, and Ellie couldn't glance away.

Her breath caught in her throat, and her lady parts started to tingle. That hadn't happened in a long, long time. What the hell was wrong with her?

The club had gone silent, the music shut off, and the male strippers melted away. Ellie blinked as one by one, the men marched to their respective women. Except him. He stood staring at her.

She forced herself to turn away and finished packing up the presents, with help from Sage, who seemed to want to steer as clear of the men as Ellie did.

"Who planned this?" Damon asked.

"That was me." Ellie turned to face Damon.

"You're the wedding planner," Max stated.

"Obviously," she muttered.

"Party planner as well," Sierra said. "Don't pick on Ellie."

"I'm not." Max shook his head. "Ellie surprised me, that's all."

"Besides it was Tessa's and my idea," Crystal said, hand on her hip.

"You and I are going to have a very long talk," Jordan promised, his voice low.

Sage coughed. "We've got the presents packed up. Max, if you give me your keys, Ellie and I will load them while you finish sorting this out."

"Sure." Max tossed his keys to Sage.

Together they gathered up the gifts and headed out. The man staring at Ellie took a step, but stopped when Sage glared at him. He held his hands up and backed away.

"That was impressive," Ellie said.

"You just need to know how to handle the Doms."

Ellie loaded the gifts while Sage ran back inside and picked up the leftover cake. "I'm heading out. Will you give Max his keys?" Sage said, dropping them in Ellie's palm.

"Sure. Night, Sage." Locking the SUV, Ellie walked back inside and joined Max and Sierra. "Everything is in the car." She held the keys out to Max. "Sage took off." Ellie turned to Sierra. "The cake needs to go into the fridge when you get home."

"I'll make sure it does." Sierra's words were slightly slurred.

How much had Sierra had to drink? Ellie wasn't sure.

"No, I'll make sure," Max said.

"Thank you, Ellie. It was a great party." Sierra hugged her, then stepped back.

"Logan," Max called out. "Can you escort Ellie home, please?"

The man who'd been staring at her joined them. "It would be my pleasure."

"I'm fine. I didn't drink and can easily get a rideshare."

"Unacceptable," Logan declared.

Ellie rolled her eyes.

"Come on, Miss Party Planner. I'll get you home." He placed his hand under her elbow.

At his touch, a spark went through Ellie's body. She allowed him to escort her out of the building. "This isn't necessary, you know." Ellie wasn't sure she wanted to be alone with the obviously dominant male.

He glanced at her. "It is." He led her to a big black SUV. "You need a ride home, and I want to make sure you get there safely."

What was it with men and their big vehicles? Ellie wasn't short by any means, but even she would need the running board to get inside this thing.

The lights flashed and the horn beeped as he unlocked it. She reached for the door handle, but he had it open before she could touch it.

"Thank you." It was nice for a man to be a gentleman. She gazed up and judged how to get into the vehicle without having her dress ride up and show off her underwear. There was a handhold right inside the door. Taking a step up onto the running board, she reached for the handhold.

"Easy." His deep voice was right next to Ellie's ear as his hands snuck around her waist, and he lifted her into the cab.

Ellie squealed. "I was fine getting in by myself." This man was taking liberties since they'd just met.

A grin played around his lips. Those full, sensual lips. "I'm sure you could, but it was easier for both of us this way." He stepped back, his gaze lingering on her legs before he pushed the door shut.

Ellie blew out a breath and fastened her seatbelt. The heat of his gaze on her legs filled her body with unwanted desire. *Don't let him get to you.* Logan climbed into the vehicle with cat-like grace and started the engine. "Where to?"

"Fourteen sixty-three Middleton Court."

"Got it." He pulled out of the parking lot. "I'm Logan Wolfe, by the way."

"Ellie Tanner."

"I know." He flashed Ellie a grin, and her lady parts tingled once again. She barely stopped her eyes from rolling.

"How do you know?" she asked.

"I saw you walking around the club with Sierra."

Of course. He was one of the club members. All of the men tonight were members of Wicked Sanctuary. Ellie shifted in her seat. Would she see him in the club if she joined? Ellie had an appointment with Max in two weeks.

She was surprised when they made it to her apartment so quickly and easily. Well, it was after midnight and traffic was light. Logan parked the vehicle at the front, near the entrance. "Wait and I'll help you out."

She opened her mouth to tell him there was no need, but the look in his eyes made her swallow her words. Ellie nodded. Was this what Sierra meant when she said the Doms used silent communication?

While he walked around the vehicle, she unbuckled her seatbelt and took a deep breath. The door opened, and she turned. Hands framed her waist and lifted her out. Her knees were slightly weak when her feet touched the ground. Why was his touch doing this to her?

"Thank you." She moved out of his hold, not liking how her body reacted. As good-looking as Logan was, she didn't have time for a man in her life. She also wasn't sure at all about the lifestyle he lived.

"I'll walk you in." He shut the door and locked the vehicle.

"You…" Her words trailed off when he looked at her. That stare. "Fine." She huffed and walked down the sidewalk to the lobby door. She punched in the code, and the door clicked. "There. I'm in."

Reaching around her, he pushed the door open and gestured for her to enter. Tiredness crept into her bones, and she didn't have the energy left to argue with him. Ellie marched to the elevator and pressed the button. When it arrived, he stepped into the small enclosure with her.

Leather and… She couldn't quite identify his scent. Ellie kept her gaze on the elevator door. Logan, for some reason, made her feel small and feminine. That was so not her. She wasn't a fragile woman.

Finally, the door opened on the tenth floor, and Ellie quickly made her way to her apartment. "Thank you. Have a good rest of your evening." She put the key in the lock.

"I need to look around."

She'd heard from the other women how protective their men were, but this was hitting her buttons. "There's no need."

"There is every need." He nudged her away and opened her door.

"Enough." Ellie stepped in front of him and lifted her chin. "I allowed you to accompany me this far; you are not going to enter my home. End of discussion. If you persist, I will call the police. We can end this encounter on friendly terms or as adversaries. Your choice."

He stared at her, and she stared right back. "I'm on the tenth floor of a secured building," she felt compelled to add.

"Doesn't mean someone can't get in." His brown eyes blazed with…anger? No. Something else. "You are a stubborn woman."

"You better believe it." She tilted her head back to meet his gaze. "Thank you for the escort, Logan. I appreciate the gesture. Good night." She gestured to the hallway.

He didn't move. For a moment, his eyes flared with fire, then it was gone. "Good night, Ellie. I'll see you another time. Lock up after me." He reached up and ran his finger over her cheek, then he turned and sauntered back to the elevator.

Ellie shut the door and threw the deadbolt as fire ran over her skin from his touch. *No, no, no.* She was so not going down this road. She didn't need a man in her life.

A giggle left her lips. She and Sierra had talked about Ellie joining Wicked Sanctuary. Wasn't that what joining the club was about? She shook her head. No, that was about releasing tensions, not about finding a man. She'd talked with both Sierra and Crystal. The club would give her a chance to explore a side of herself she'd always been curious about. That's all it was. With a sigh, she pulled away from the door and headed for her bedroom.

One thing she did know: She'd stay clear of Logan in the club. The man was too intense. Too serious. She wanted to have some fun, not be ordered around.

Another shiver raced through her as she thought about Logan's commanding air and penetrating gaze. She didn't want intense.

Right?

Chapter 2

Two weeks later, Ellie parked her car in the lot and sat there. Wicked Sanctuary. Even though she'd been here before to chat with Sierra and Max about their wedding, this was different. Tonight, she planned to become a member. Well, at least she hoped to. And sitting out here in her car wasn't getting her into the club.

She climbed out of her vehicle and walked up to the door with WS carved into it and knocked. The door swung open.

"Right on time, come on in," Max said.

"Thank you." Ellie scooted past him. Max was dressed casually in a pair of soft looking pants, a black shirt, and loafers. "Am I dressed okay?" She'd come directly from work and was still in a skirt and heels.

"For tonight, yes." He gestured for her to precede him down the hall.

They passed a large set of double doors, the bathrooms, another doorway, and entered the office at the end of hallway.

"You're the only applicant tonight, so I figured we could be a little more informal." Max gestured to the chair in front of his desk.

"I could come back another night." She wasn't sure if it was a good sign or not to be the only one there.

"It's fine. Tonight is really about paperwork and rules."

"Okay." Ellie sat down, setting her purse next to her leg. "I hope you and Sierra had a good honeymoon." She hadn't talked with Sierra since they got back.

"We did." He grinned. "Why don't we dive right in. Why do you want to join Wicked Sanctuary, Ellie?"

"I need someplace to relax." She wasn't surprised by the question. Sierra had told her about the classes and the first night; Max would make sure she was a good fit. He regarded her with dark eyes.

"How much do you know about the lifestyle?"

"A little." She'd done some research, but not a lot. "If you count reading erotic romances as research."

Max grinned. "Depends. They can be good or bad." He pushed a folder across the table to her. "Why don't you fill out the first couple forms. Also, we do a complete background check. Are you okay with that?"

"Of course." There was nothing in her background to be ashamed of. Unless they counted a divorce and parents who'd been married several times over. She opened the folder and began filling out the paperwork while Max looked over some work of his own.

The NDA and information needed for a background check. Those were easy. Although she found it interesting about the NDA. It was really to protect other members, not the club itself. She closed the folder and handed it back to Max.

"Thank you." He glanced over the paperwork in the folder and handed her another one. "This one has your application, club rules, and a detailed questionnaire you might need to take home to complete."

Ellie nodded. She opened the folder. Name, date of birth, phone number, emergency contact, gender identity, preferred pronouns. Those were easy. Next choice: Dom, Submissive, Switch, Unsure.

She nibbled on her nail, then circled *Unsure*. She'd read about male and female Doms and submissives, but she wasn't sure she could order someone around or allow someone to order her around. That was the part that worried her the most.

The next form was a liability disclaimer, and then Bylaws. Initialed and dated.

Club rules. Four pages of rules. She'd never remember them all, but she started reading. No cell phones or electronics allowed in the club.

She looked up. "What do we do with our phones and purses while we're in the club?"

"Sierra showed you the bathroom, right? There are lockers there you'll secure your things."

She'd forgotten about seeing them. That was good to know. She kept reading, most were straightforward. Initialed and dated.

She flipped to the next page. The questionnaire. Her heart stuttered. There were…she counted…twelve pages? Ellie glanced at her watch. She'd been here at seven on the dot, and it was now a few minutes after eight. There was no way she'd get through this questionnaire tonight.

Ellie read the instructions twice: Choices were yes, no, and unsure. If the applicant circled no, they were to note hard or soft. Okay that shouldn't be too hard. She started with the first question. Anal play. Her face heated. Maybe this wasn't such a good idea.

"Are you okay, Ellie?"

She jumped at Max's voice. "Ummm…"

He sat back in his chair. "Didn't mean to scare you."

"It's okay."

"Are you having trouble with the questionnaire?"

How the hell did he know that? *Probably because my face is the color of a dark red rose.* "I wasn't expecting something so detailed."

He nodded. "The questionnaire is the hardest part of the process. You need to be honest with yourself. Don't shy away from your needs and desires."

What if she had no clue what her needs and desires were? She bit her lower lip so she didn't blurt the question out. Squirming in her chair, she wondered if she should just forget this whole thing. Maybe this wasn't a good idea.

"Don't overthink this," Max said.

Ellie's eyes widened. Was the man a mind-reader?

Max smiled. "I've worked with both men and women who worry this lifestyle isn't for them. I'll tell you the same thing I've told them: The only way to know for sure is to give it a try." He paused, watching her intently. "I take it you finished all the other forms?"

"Oh yes." She took them out of the folder and handed them to him.

"I've said you might need to take the questionnaire home; why don't you do that? Sometimes it's easier in a more relaxed setting."

Ellie blew out a breath. Maybe he was right. "Okay."

"The background check takes a week or so. I'll give you a call once it's back, and I've approved you. Then we'll set you up for the second class."

"Can you remind me what the classes are?"

"Certainly. Tonight is basically paperwork. Class two is protocols in the club. I'll give you a copy of your paperwork, answer any questions you might have, and take your questionnaire responses."

"Who sees the questionnaires?" Ellie couldn't stand the idea that her intimate answers would be fodder for anyone in the club to read, especially the Dom who'd driven her home after the bachelorette party. She already couldn't get Logan out of her mind. If he read her questionnaire…

"Only me and your mentor, at first. If you work with someone else besides your mentor, that person will need to review your hard and soft limits."

She nodded.

"You'll also meet your training mentor next week."

"Training mentor?" Ellie's nerves ratcheted back up again. Sierra hadn't said anything about that.

"Yes. Everyone has a training mentor to help them navigate their first few times through the club."

"Who will mine be?"

"I don't know yet." Max rubbed his chin. "With a lot of us Doms in relationships and preferring not to mentor a new member, I have to find a suitable Dom for you."

"Ah…Max I'm not sure if I'm a Dom, submissive, or switch."

"I saw that you checked the unsure box. Don't worry. We're used to that here, and once you finish the questionnaire, we'll talk about it. Can you trust me to find you the perfect mentor?"

She thought for a moment. "Yes, Max. I trust you to find me the right mentor." It was the right choice to make.

"Thank you. Take that home and fill it out. If you get it done before I call you with the results of the background check, scan, password protect it, and email it to me." He handed her a business card with his name and email address on it. "Once I receive it, I'll call you for the password."

"I will." Clutching the folder to her chest, she snagged her purse and stood, more than ready to leave. "This has been eye opening."

Max smiled. "I'm sure it has. I want you to feel comfortable here, Ellie. We all need a place to relax and be ourselves." Max escorted her to her car and waited until she was on her way before he went back inside.

Ellie thought about his words on the way home. A place to relax, let go, and be herself. Outside of her apartment, she hadn't found a place like that in a long time, if ever. Her pulse spiked in anticipation. Now she was excited to fill out the questionnaire and get this show on the road.

* * * *

Logan Wolfe grabbed a beer out of the fridge and plopped down on the sofa. Four days of freedom. He laughed. He loved his job as a police officer, but the long days were starting to get to him.

He was off until Monday morning, and he couldn't wait to go to the club and relax around friends and maybe play with a sub or two. With all the extra shifts he'd taken on, and schedules being changed often, it had been a while since he'd been able to play.

There was also the fact that lately, something had been missing for him, and he didn't have a damn clue what that was. Was it because he didn't have a woman in his life? He shook his head. He'd promised himself a long time ago he wouldn't go into a relationship while he was a cop. His job was volatile, and he wouldn't risk leaving a woman he cared about to mourn him. His cell rang, and he glanced at the display.

"Hey, Max," Logan said. That man had a way of knowing when to call.

"Logan, I was wondering if I could ask a big favor."

"Sure. What's up?" Logan took a long drink of his beer.

"I've got a new sub coming in tomorrow, and I was hoping you could mentor her."

"Me?" Logan was surprised. Max usually asked one of the other Doms in the club.

"Yes. Her questionnaire matched up almost perfectly with yours."

"I've never done it before, and you know my work schedule is unpredictable."

"I know, but it will only be for the next three Thursdays. Do you think you can swing it?"

Logan thought about his schedule. "Yeah, I think so." Most the time, he avoided the night shift, and even if he worked twelve-hour days, he should be done by seven at night. It would be tight to get to the club by eight, but he could make it work.

"Great. Can you start tomorrow and meet your mentee."

"You got lucky; I'm off until Monday."

"Wonderful. Come at seven, and I'll introduce you. You're going to be great."

Logan shook his head after Max disconnected. He hoped he would be as good as Max thought he'd be. Flipping on the TV, he found a football game and relaxed on his sofa. He wondered what Ellie was doing tonight. The curvy, feisty brunette hadn't left his thoughts much since the night of Sierra's bachelorette party. It was unusual for a woman to take up space in his mind. Maybe it was because the last few months had been busy, and he hadn't had a chance to let off steam at the club?

Or maybe it was the way she rolled her eyes at him or the death glare from those stunning blue eyes. His cock twitched. Yeah, that was another thing. Damn cock had it bad for Ellie even though he'd just met her.

Maybe he'd get her contact information from Sierra. He'd tried to find her, but he couldn't find a party planning place with her name, and he wouldn't abuse his official position to search police databases. He grinned. Yeah, tomorrow night he'd chat with Sierra.

Chapter 3

Logan strode into Wicked Sanctuary a few minutes after seven Thursday night. For some reason, traffic had been heavier than he'd expected. "Evening, Ralph," he said, signing in.

"Logan." Ralph was a staple of the club. He'd been behind the reception desk for as long as Logan had been a member. "Max is waiting in the classroom for you."

"Thanks." Max hadn't said what the dress code was, so Logan kept it casual. T-shirt, lightweight cotton material pants, and loafers. If he was going into the club later, it would be easy enough to strip his shirt off.

"Oh good, you're here," Max said as he walked into the room right behind Logan.

"Hey, Max." Logan's gaze took in the room, and he was surprised to see only one person sitting there. Jordan had mentioned they usually had classes of four to six. He blinked. Ellie?

"You remember Ellie from Sierra's bachelorette party?"

"Yes." Logan smiled. This was interesting. Ellie stared at him, her blue eyes giving nothing away, but the color in her cheeks was telling.

"I've already explained the protocols to Ellie, so this is a good time for the two of you to go over the questionnaire together."

"Sounds good to me," Logan said. In one way, he was blown away to see Ellie here, and in another, not. At least now, he didn't have to ask Sierra for her information. Wait a second. He hadn't seen her background check come through. Max always had him to do those; he must have had one of the others do it. There were several officers who frequented the club.

"Ellie?"

She blinked several times. "Uh, sure."

Logan strode over and sat down next to her as Max walked out of the room. "So we meet again."

"Yes." Her voice was soft.

Tonight, her brunette hair was pulled back, and she wore minimal makeup. His gaze roamed over her clothing. A lightweight shirt, jeans, and sneakers. His dick took notice of how beautiful she looked, but it was more than that. She was here, and he was her mentor. He almost rubbed his hands together, thinking about how much fun they would have. *Slow down. She's new to the lifestyle.* Or was she?

"Do you mentor often?" she asked, her words soft.

"My first time." He would be completely honest with her.

"Oh. Have you been a member for a while?"

"I have. What made you want to join?" He wanted to know more about this intriguing woman.

"I wanted a place where I could relax and be me." She shifted in the chair, her fingers toying with the folder sitting in front of her.

"Is that your questionnaire?"

She nodded.

"May I?" He held his hand out for it.

She clutched the pages, crushing the corners. "Before we go too deep into this, I need to ask you a few questions."

Logan sat back in the chair. Good for her. She was going to make sure they were a right fit, or at minimum, satisfy some curiosity. "Go for it."

"What do you do?"

"I'm a police officer with the Pleasant Valley PD."

She stiffened. "You're a cop?"

"Is that a problem?"

"I…" She pushed back her chair and stood. "Excuse me." Ellie rushed out of the room, leaving her folder and purse on the table. He stood, but stopped himself from going after her. Something about him being a cop had set her off, not the fact he was in the lifestyle. Interesting.

"Where's Ellie?" Max asked, coming back into the classroom.

"She just rushed out of here." Logan blew out a breath. "Did you see anything in her background check that would make her biased against cops?"

Max shook his head. "She ran because you're a police officer?"

"We were chatting; she asked what I did, and I told her. She ran out, leaving her purse and folder here."

Max frowned. "You didn't follow?"

"No. Max, one thing I've learned is not to go after a woman when she runs away after hearing what my job is."

"I'll go check on her."

"Thanks." Logan was usually more prepared for a woman's rejection. It had happened before when he mentioned his job. But Ellie's stung. As much as he wanted to play with her, he would have to accept her decision. His job was his job.

Ellie walked back into the room, Max right behind her. "Sorry," she said as she sat down. "What I ate for lunch didn't agree with me."

"Are you okay to continue?" Max asked.

"If you're not well, we can do this tomorrow night," Logan said. He didn't like that she wasn't feeling well. He suspected it was something more. He'd eventually figure it out.

"I'm good." Her tummy growled, and she ducked her head.

Logan glanced at Max and made a quick decision. "Do you feel up to some soup? I know a great little place, and we can still discuss the questionnaire."

"Is that allowed?" She glanced at Max.

"Go," he said. "Ellie, you need to know that I trust Logan. I also trust you to make the right choice for you. There's no right or wrong here."

Logan stood and held his hand out to her. He thought for a moment she would refuse, but she put her hand in his. Her skin was cool to the touch. "Thanks, Max."

Logan escorted her out of the club. "Since we both have vehicles, why don't you follow me."

"Okay." She walked over to her small car, and Logan waited until she got in before heading to his vehicle. He backed out and made sure she was behind him before he pulled out. Once they were on their way to town, he realized he should have gotten her cell number in case they got separated.

But Ellie was very careful and stayed close. He pulled into the J & I Soup and Sandwich parking lot, a little hole-in-the-wall place he'd found a couple of months ago. It was run by a family that made the best soup and sandwiches.

He met Ellie at her car and was pleased she remembered to grab her folder. Keeping his hand on her elbow, he guided her into the small restaurant. "Logan." Julie hugged him.

"Julie." Logan hugged her back. "This is my friend, Ellie. Do you by chance have a table for us?"

"For you, always." Julie glanced at Ellie. "Welcome, Ellie." Julie waved her hand for them to follow.

"Come here a lot?" Ellie asked.

"Quite a bit." Logan held the chair out for Ellie.

"Thank you." She sat down and placed the folder on the table.

Logan took the seat across from her. Ellie was very quiet, and he tried not to let it bother him. But she was hiding something, and he wondered what it was.

"Logan," Ian said, walking up to the table. "And who is this beautiful woman?"

"Ian." Logan grinned. "This is Ellie. Ellie, Ian, the other half of J & I Soup and Sandwich."

"It's very nice to meet you."

"You too. Logan's never brought a woman here before. We are honored."

Ellie's cheeks turned pink. She was blushing again. What did that mean? Logan wondered if she was embarrassed by Ian's words, or was it something else? Would she blush in the club? *Don't get ahead of yourself.*

"What would you like to drink?" Ian asked.

"Water for me, please," Ellie said.

"Soda."

"Got it. Our special is chicken and rice soup with fresh sourdough bread. Be right back with your drinks." Ian walked away.

"Ellie, if you're not feeling up to this, we can do it another night." He didn't want her to feel obligated.

"I'll be fine. I just need to eat something to settle my stomach." Her voice was soft, and her gaze didn't quite meet his.

Logan kept his gaze on her, wondering if maybe Max's radar on matching Doms and subs was off. Ian came back with their drinks and took their order.

Ellie took a long drink of her water. Logan kept his gaze on her. While the color in her face was better, she still wasn't a hundred percent.

"You mentioned you joined Wicked Sanctuary so you could be you. What did you mean by that?"

She tilted her head and bit her lip. "I want people to see me, not Ellie the party planner."

He sensed there was more. "What else?"

She glanced away from him. "A place to relax."

"And?" He wasn't going to let her off the hook.

"What makes you think there's more?"

There was that spark. Was that what he was digging for? Maybe. He wanted to see her eyes flash at him. To see the spunky side he'd seen the night he drove her home. "I can tell. You need to be honest with me, Ellie. It's the only way this will work."

Her hand fluttered to her chest. "I know." She sighed. "This isn't easy for me." She fiddled with the collar of her shirt. "I think I want to feel connected." There was that softness again. Logan wasn't yet positive what that said about her true feelings, but he was getting closer.

"I can understand that." Connection was a big part of Wicked Sanctuary, being with likeminded people. "How much do you know about the lifestyle?"

She pushed the folder across the table. Her hand lingered on the report before she pulled back and rested her hand in her lap. "I'm new to it. I've done a little research, but nothing major. I talked with Sierra before I made the appointment to apply."

Logan nodded and opened the folder. There was a sticky note from Max. He read it quickly, then moved on to her questionnaire. Max had been right; her kinks were similar to his. But the sticky note intrigued him. Max had written: *She's not sure if she's a sub or switch. I really can't see her as a Dominant but can see her topping from the bottom at times.*

Interesting. Ellie did have a strong personality. Yet there was something he couldn't put his finger on. Her surprise at seeing him wasn't unexpected.

"Are you okay with me being your mentor?"

"Why wouldn't I be?"

There she went answering a question with a question. Was she trying to divert the conversation away from the hard topics? Time for a new tactic. "You weren't exactly happy with me the night I drove you home from Sierra's bachelorette party."

"You were bossy."

He laughed. "I hate to tell you, but I'm always bossy." He was a Dominant through and through, and his need to protect steered him to law enforcement.

"I don't like taking orders."

"I noticed. You know, BDSM isn't about one person ordering another one around."

"It's not?"

"No. It's a give and take." He tried to think of a way to explain it. He'd been in the lifestyle for a while, but this was the first time he'd taken on a completely novice sub. He studied her for a minute. "Tell me: How did you feel in your gut when I told you to wait while I made sure your apartment was safe the night I took you home?"

Her shoulders relaxed. "In my gut, protected. In my head, frustrated."

"Why frustrated?"

"Because it's important to me to take care of myself."

"Understood, but your gut said protected. That's the feeling I want to give you. That any Dom should give you." He'd felt compelled to add that last bit, but Logan already knew no other Dom would be playing with Ellie while he was around.

"I don't understand."

At least she wasn't telling him it wasn't going to work. "I'm probably botching this up, but for me and the way I was taught, the Dom/sub relationship is a give and take. I want a sub I can protect and keep safe, but also one I can make feel good about her body and give her pleasure. Pleasure designed for her only."

Ellie sat there staring at him. Had he revealed too much? He didn't think so. He'd heard the Doms talking at their meetings. Besides, if he was going to be her mentor, that meant showing her who he was.

"I never thought of it that way. What do you get out of it? You talk about me but not you."

"I receive my pleasure from you. By that, I mean, when you're happy and satisfied, so am I."

She bit her lower lip before answering. "I don't know. Maybe Sierra was wrong when she said I belonged at Wicked Sanctuary."

"Why?" Sierra was a good judge of character from what he'd seen, and Max could weed out those who weren't suited for the lifestyle before they got to this part.

Ellie shrugged. "I'm not sure I'm submissive material."

"That's why we talk before we do anything. Have you ever wanted to hand control over to someone else?"

"No."

She answered quickly, and Logan realized his mistake. "I phrased that wrong. Have you ever wanted to give control over in the bedroom?"

Her eyes softened. "Yes."

"That's what I'm talking about."

"You don't want to control my business?"

"No, I don't. That would be a 24/7 Dom/sub relationship. Going that far would involve total power exchange; that's not me. For me, this is about what a submissive wants in the bedroom or when we are together in the club. Does the sub want the Dom to take the lead? Does the sub want the Dom to tie them up and tease them? Does the sub want the Dom to make their most erotic fantasies come true?"

As he spoke, she kept her attention on him, and her body relaxed. She was letting go of her inhibitions and listening to him. A warm fuzzy feeling went through his blood.

"I'd like that." Her voice was strong.

"Good. I don't want to take over your life."

Ellie shook her head. "But…" She sighed. "Maybe I've been reading the wrong books."

"It's possible. Are you okay with me being your mentor?"

"I'd like to know more about you. You're a police officer?"

"Yes." The caution was back in her eyes. "Is that going to be a problem?"

She paused, then shook her head. "It will be fine."

Logan didn't quite believe her, but he'd let it go for now. They needed to get past the first few scenes, either private or in the club, before he made any decision about a relationship outside the club. Oh, yes, he was definitely intrigued, and finding out what she wanted was the icing on the cake.

"All right, I haven't read your complete questionnaire yet, but I know we're compatible based on what I saw on the first page. What I'd like to talk about is how you feel about us being seen together?"

"What do you mean? In the club? Everyone has to sign an NDA, don't they?"

"Yes. I mean like what we're doing right now. Outside the club. While you're in training, my job is to get you used to the club and help you feel comfortable in the space, but it's hard to do that unless I get to know you. And for me to do that, I need to see you outside of club space." He'd heard the other Doms talk about how important it was to develop at least a friendship with their mentee. Several of the Doms went on to have relationships with them, and he wanted that with Ellie. Friendship was fine, but not a permanent relationship that could lead to marriage. He couldn't risk that with his job, but a nice friends-with-benefits thing that gave them both some companionship and sex.

* * * *

Ellie stared at Logan. Just her luck. The man who lit up her libido like a Christmas tree was a cop. How could she be with a man who risked his life on a daily basis? A shiver went through her as she remembered seeing her brother lying lifeless. No.

She should ask for another mentor. Max would make it happen, but she had a sneaking suspicion he'd want to know why. She wasn't ready to talk about her reasons. Not yet. Would she ever be ready? Maybe one day.

Okay, she could make this work. It was only for a short period of time. She wasn't going to lose her heart to a cop. She'd keep her emotions on lockdown.

Ian brought their dinner. She'd ordered the special, and it smelled heavenly. Logan had asked Ian for his usual, and Ellie glanced at his plate. Not only was there a bowl of soup, but a mile-high French dip along with a pile of french fries.

"You must be hungry," Ellie observed before dipping her spoon into the soup.

"I am." He didn't pick up his spoon or his sandwich. Instead, his gaze was on her as she sipped her soup.

Her eyes widened. The chicken practically melted in her mouth, and the broth was delicious. "That is fantastic."

Logan grinned. "They have the best here."

"I never knew this place existed." Maybe because she'd been so busy lately, she barely had time to run to Sweet & Savory to grab food, and today she'd ordered from a place close to her shop. And looked what happened there. The fish and chips hadn't settled well in her stomach. Now, she was starving, but she'd be smart to stick to the soup and bread. By tomorrow, she'd be right as rain.

She watched him eat. The man did everything like it was his only focus, yet she knew he also saw everything around him. Logan had asked her about seeing him outside the club, and she hadn't answered him.

Maybe because she didn't know. She was already attracted to him. Could she see him socially and not make it look like some big relationship? The mentorship was only three weeks, although Max said many kept the relationship going until the pair agreed to part. She would not be able to stay with Logan beyond the mentorship. The man was as dangerous to her peace of mind as his job was to him.

She had to wonder how many of the women found the men they loved through this mentorship program. No, she couldn't think like that. She'd trusted her ex and learned the hard way she was better off without a man in her life. Even if she decided to consider another relationship, it wouldn't be with a police officer.

Wait… Wasn't that why she'd joined Wicked Sanctuary? To be with a man? To explore her sensuality that she'd suppressed with her ex. Ellie rolled her eyes. No, the ex didn't belong in her thoughts. Period.

"You rolled your eyes. What's going on in that head of yours?" Logan asked.

Had he been watching her this whole time? Ellie shook her head. "Nothing."

She smiled and went back to her meal, but Logan pressed on. "You never answered my question about seeing me outside the club."

"I think I can do that. It's really going to depend on my schedule and yours." She had no idea what kind of hours he worked. Maybe that would give her an out or at least curtail their time together.

"I understand. As a party planner, do you attend all the parties you set up?"

"Oh Lord, no. Sierra's was a special case since I was doing the wedding reception the next day. Most of the time, I make sure everything is set up and check in with my workers by text to make sure everything is going well."

"I'm glad you were there, or we wouldn't have met."

A shiver slid over her spine, and Ellie tamped it down. "The group of you were very imposing."

Logan laughed. "The guys weren't too happy to find their women at a strip club."

"Hey, it wasn't a strip club. The Oasis is a very respectable…okay, strip club. But the men were never nude."

"Thank goodness, or Max would have flipped out." Logan rubbed his chin. "Come to think of it, so would the other guys. They all had wives and girlfriends there."

"But you didn't?" The question slipped from her lips before she could censor it.

He shook his head. "Nope. And now I'm glad. So, Miss Party Planner, dinner tomorrow night, and I'll check with Max if it's okay to take you to the club. Not to play, but to observe."

Ellie shook her head. She pulled her phone out of her purse and pulled up her calendar. "Sorry, I have a retirement party tomorrow night at seven."

"You don't have help?"

"I do have two people on contract, but they're doing other events for me tomorrow."

"Saturday night?"

"Two birthday parties and a baby shower, but I should be done by five."

"Let's plan for me to pick you up at six."

"I can drive myself."

"Remember what I said? Protective."

Ellie shook her head. "It's going to take me a bit to understand that. Besides, it doesn't make sense for you to drive to my apartment, then to dinner, then back to my apartment. Where do you live by the way?"

"Off of Jackson."

"Isn't that the new housing development being built by Riggs Construction?" She remembered seeing information about the models out there. She'd actually toured one, but she wasn't sure she needed a house right now. Her apartment was fine.

"It is. Zeke is a friend, and he found me the perfect place."

"That means you'll have to double back to my apartment." She shook her head. "I'll drive myself."

Warm fingers captured hers. Logan had reached across the table and placed his fingers over hers. "Let me do this, Ellie."

"Okay." She sighed, not wanting to argue with him. "But I won't always be this amendable."

Logan grinned. "You'll be surprised."

An hour later she was. Logan followed her home and walked her inside her apartment building, checked her apartment, and left her with a kiss on the cheek.

Her surprise wasn't that she'd let him check her apartment, it was the heat from that little kiss on the cheek. It flowed through her veins and straight to her core. Wasn't it a plus she was attracted to the man she was going to be with at the club?

She pushed away from her front door and made her way into her bedroom. Thank goodness she had fresh batteries in her vibrator; she was going to need it tonight.

Chapter 4

Logan stepped from the bathroom into his bedroom and glanced at the clock. Five. Ellie would be leaving work about now. He'd talked to her earlier in the day and told her Max approved of her going to the club tonight, so she should make sure she had the appropriate clothing.

He'd already thrown his club clothes into his bag. By the time he was finished dressing, it was time to leave. On the drive, he thought once again about Thursday night with Ellie. She was so new to the lifestyle. He'd spoken with Max about it, and Max reminded him that most of the subs, including his wife, had been new at some point.

Max was right. Logan hadn't been a mentor before and was afraid of messing things up. Max told him to do what felt right with Ellie, and the mentor relationship didn't have to end when the classes did. Most kept it going for at least a couple three to four weeks after the mentorship ended until the sub felt comfortable on their own.

Logan blew out a breath. The question was: Could he let Ellie go at the end of that time? Yeah, he had it bad. Ellie tugged at something inside him, and he wanted to wrap her in his arms and protect her. Was it because he was a cop? He didn't think so. He'd never felt this strongly about a woman before.

He wasn't sure if she was aware or not, but he watched her at Sierra's wedding and reception. While she tried to keep to the background, Sierra and the other women dragged her out onto the dance floor and into their circle. It was good that she had these friends.

Pulling into a parking spot, Logan climbed out of his SUV, made his way to her apartment building entrance, and pressed the button for her apartment. He liked this building, good security, and it was well maintained.

Ellie's voice came over the speaker. "I'll be right down, Logan." And the speaker clicked off before he could respond.

He crossed his arms over his chest and waited. Soon, she came bouncing out the door with a smile on her face, her hair pulled back, and a bag in her hand. He took the bag from her, set it down, and cupped her shoulders. "Why did you make me wait outside?"

Ellie stared at him. "Did I make you wait too long?"

"No." He took a breath. "Why didn't you let me come in? I need to understand." He wasn't angry, just confused.

Her cheeks turned pink. "I didn't think about it."

Logan thought about her words. "I like to escort my dates. That means I pick you up at your apartment door and drop you off there at the end of the night. It's how I was raised."

She tilted her head. "I'm not used to that."

He stared at her. "Not used to it? Get used to it. I take care of my…mentees."

"Look, Logan—"

Logan worked to keep his impatience from getting the better of him. It would take time and effort to find a middle ground, especially with Ellie. "No. You need to understand here and now that I want to protect you, and I will do so for as long as we're together. If you can't live with that, maybe I'm not the right mentor for you. Although, I believe any Dom would feel the same way."

When she didn't answer, he picked up her bag and cupped her elbow.

Ellie pulled away. "Look, Logan. If it's going to be a lecture every time I do something you don't like, maybe I should ask Max to assign someone else as my mentor."

"You will not." Why did he say that after telling her that maybe he wasn't the right mentor for her? Maybe because he needed her to understand this was going to take compromise on both sides.

She closed her eyes, then opened them. "I'm not going to argue with you, but understand this: I am my own woman. If I choose to meet you instead of buzzing you inside, I see that as a courtesy. Why make you come all the way to my apartment when I can easily save you the trip."

Logan fought against his dominant side. It was a struggle. "I get it." He did. Compromise. "Please understand that is not part of my makeup."

"How about we meet half-way, you can escort me to my apartment at the end of our evening to start with?"

"I can do that." It wouldn't be easy, but he wouldn't tolerate another Dom as her mentor. He wasn't planning to let her go, at least not until their relationship came to a mutual conclusion and when he wasn't so damned attracted to her.

Logan gestured for her to precede him to his vehicle. "I did warn you I had a protective side, and sometimes it gets the better of me."

"I get it. I just wasn't expecting it on our first outing together."

"I'm glad you didn't hold back with me. If I do something that upsets you, tell me about it. You had no problem telling me off that night I drove you home from the bachelorette party. And you did allow me to check your apartment out the other night."

Her lips twitched. "Deal. As long as you're willing to really listen to what I have to say."

"Done."

Logan opened the door, helped her into his vehicle, then stowed her bag in the back.

"Where are we going for dinner?" she asked as he drove away from her building.

"I was thinking The Aztec Chef. Does that work?"

"Yes." Traffic was light, so they made it to the restaurant in record time and were able to place their order right away.

"How will tonight work?" Ellie asked.

"Since you're a novice, all we will do is walk around so you can get a feel for the club. I do have to warn you: it's Saturday night, so it will be busy with a lot of scenes going on."

"That makes sense. Max said the club is only open Thursday through Saturday." The waiter placed a bowl of chips in front of them, along with their drinks.

"Yes, Fridays and Saturdays are very busy. Thursdays are for classes, if there are any, and demos for those who like to play on less crowded nights." He watched her pick up a chip and dip it in the salsa. As her lips closed over the chip, his dick took notice.

Settle down; we've seen women eat before. But there was something sensual about the way Ellie bit into the chip, chewed, and swallowed. She relished each bite. If she turned that focus on him, this woman would be lethal.

"We're not going to do anything tonight?"

"We won't. As I said, you can get a feel for the club, watch a few scenes, and we can discuss how the scenes make you feel."

Ellie bit her lower lip. "Discuss? What do you mean? I'm not sure there would be much to talk about."

Logan bit back a smile. "A lot of what we will discuss is around what you're seeing, what you're feeling, and if it's something you want to try."

"Max didn't mention that." She took another chip.

"He must have forgotten. He did go over the protocols with you, didn't he?"

"Yes. Never interrupt a scene. All Doms are Sir. Red is my safeword, and if something doesn't look right, tell one of the dungeon masters, and they will check it out."

"Good. Also, there is a bar, but alcohol isn't served."

"Right. Why is that?"

"Alcohol and kink don't mix well. Mistakes are made."

"Is that why you're not drinking tonight?"

"You're not either."

Ellie flashed a grin, one that shot straight to his cock.

"I wanted to keep a clear head tonight," she said.

Logan nodded. "I might have a beer with dinner before going to the club, but that would be about it."

"You said mistakes are made; what do you mean?"

"There's the obvious. Alcohol lowers inhibition and interferes with coordination. However, the most important point is that BDSM is about consent. When someone has consumed alcohol, they are essentially impaired and cannot give consent. No clear headed consent, no playing. I'll explain more when we get to the club. Just know I won't touch you if you're drunk or if I am."

Ellie nodded. "Okay, so we walk around, watch and talk. What else?"

"That's really it, unless you want things to go further."

"And by that you mean…"

"Touching, caressing, kissing. You do remember the dress code?"

Her cheeks turned pink. "Yep."

"What will you be wearing?" He was curious.

"You'll see." The pink in her cheeks deepened.

That was interesting. "You do realize other people will see you?" Her eyes grew wide. "I see you didn't consider that."

"No, I didn't." She frowned.

"The NDAs are there for a reason. You'll see everything at the club including full nudity. I'm sure Max told you."

"He did, I just didn't think…" She broke off as their dinner was delivered. He waited until the waiter walked away, then he reached across the table and placed his hand on top of hers.

"If you don't feel comfortable tonight, let me know, and we'll leave."

She nodded. "You said you haven't mentored before. Why not?" She dug into her food, and he did likewise.

"Max has never asked me. Usually, there are a couple of unattached Doms in the club who'll take on the duties, but they've been dropping like flies lately."

"You mean they've been hooking up with their subs."

"Yes, though this is not a dating service." He waved his fork in the air. "Some Doms will play with different subs, depending on their kink preferences. This is why the questionnaire is so important."

"It's very thorough."

"It's meant to be. Finding the right Dom can be tricky. That's the reason Max has the mentor program for all new people. It allows you to explore while being totally safe. Many of the subs stay with the mentor for months after the classes are done."

"Oh?"

"Actually, a lot of them lately have fallen for their Doms. Max and Sierra were like that."

"I'm sure theirs was an unusual case."

"Let's see, Crystal and Jordan. Damon and Tessa, although Tessa was already a member. Colby and Lara, Zeke and Allyson, Gabriel and Dani, but Dani was already a member. Then there was Anthony and Kaley, but Kaley had already gone through the classes with another member. Rose and Oliver were both already members, as were Regina and Dane. He was new, but Max and Dane knew each other in the community, so his classes were waived."

"Wow, I didn't realize."

"I'm happy for all of them. It's not easy to find someone who gets you."

"No, it's not." She put her fork down.

Logan glanced at his plate, surprised to see he'd eaten over half of his food as they chatted.

"Have you ever been married, Logan?"

"No. You?"

"Yes. I'm divorced."

It took him a moment to digest that piece of information. "What happened?" Ellie stayed silent. "You don't have to tell me." What had her ex done to her? Was that why she was worried he'd take control of her business, her life?

"We never should have gotten married." Her voice was quiet. "It was a mistake from day one."

"I'm sorry to hear that. Was this a recent divorce?" She was skittish and that could be the reason.

"No. It's been over eight years. I wanted you to know."

"Eight years." That surprised him. "You would have been eighteen?"

A giggle escaped her lips. "I was twenty-one when we divorced. We'd only been married a little over three years. Like I said, we never should have gotten married."

"Why did you?" He was curious why she married so young.

Ellie glanced away and then back. "We were too young, not enough experience. I knew within days of us marrying, we shouldn't have done it."

"Yet you stayed together." His parents had a long, loving marriage until his father died. Even now, his mother didn't pressure him to marry. Date, yes, but not marry.

"We tried to make it work. We had different goals in life."

He had a feeling there was more to it. Her body had gone stiff and her movements jerky. "Makes sense. Did you grow up here in Pleasant Valley?"

"Next town over, but I didn't spend a lot of time in Pleasant Valley. What about you?"

"Yeah, born and raised here. My mom is living with my sister in Virginia."

"That's far." She toyed with her fork. "What does your sister do in Virginia?"

"She works on Capitol Hill." His sister had decided she could make changes from the inside rather than going into law enforcement. She was good at what she did.

"That's nice." Ellie sat back in her seat. "Why did you choose law enforcement?"

Logan suspected that was the question she wanted to ask first, but didn't. "My father was in law enforcement as was my grandfather."

"Family tradition?"

He shook his head. "Yes, but my parents let me know it was my choice what I wanted as a career. I like figuring out puzzles, and law enforcement was an opportunity to do that. Do you have any brothers or sisters?"

She lowered her lashes but not before he saw a flash of pain in her eyes.

"I had a brother. He died a few years ago."

"I'm so sorry."

"Thank you. It still hurts."

"Were you close?"

Her lips turned up. "We drove my parents crazy. What I didn't think up, Tommy did."

"Sounds like me and my sister, even though there's five years between us."

"Tommy was three years older than me." She let out a sigh.

"Why did you become a party planner?" He hated the sad look on her face.

"By accident." Her features brightened. "I loved having parties when I was a kid. I'd work with my mom and plan everything out. After my divorce, I was at a loss what to do, and a friend asked me to plan her wedding shower."

"I watched you at Sierra's reception; you're very good at what you do."

Her cheeks pinkened again. "Thank you. I had fun with it. Some things were a little unconventional, but I kind of enjoy variety."

Logan filed that away for future reference. He'd have to make sure and change things up regularly when they played.

"From what you told me of your schedule, you seem very busy."

"It can be. Most of my business is word of mouth. I generally have at least a couple of birthday parties a week, be it adult or kids."

"I know you do wedding receptions and bachelorette parties, what else?"

"Just about any type of party people want to throw."

"That must keep you on your toes."

"It does at times. I had a few people come in and want me to throw parties for their animals too."

He threw his head back and laughed. "Did you do it?"

"Yes. It was fun, and animals are sometimes easier than kids."

Logan grinned, then looked at his watch. "We better get going." He waved at their waiter. "Check please."

"Of course, sir. Would you like any of the food boxed up?"

Logan looked at Ellie, and she shook her head. He'd finished his plate, but there was a little bit left on hers. "We're good."

"Very well." The waiter whisked the plates away and was back quickly with the check. Logan paid the bill and escorted Ellie out of the restaurant.

"How long have you been a member of Wicked Sanctuary?" she asked as he drove out of town.

"A while now. I joined about a year after Max opened the club." He glanced over at her, then back at the road. "Just a reminder: Tonight is for you to get the feel for the club. To look around and watch some scenes. I'll answer any questions you have."

"What scenes can I expect tonight?" She twisted her hands together in her lap.

"It depends. Usually some flogging scenes, bondage, it all depends on who's in the club." He reached over and placed his hand over hers. "Nervous?"

"A bit."

"I promise I won't leave you alone." Logan turned down the driveway to Wicked Sanctuary. At the gate, he punched in the code and then drove in. As he suspected, there were a lot of cars in the lot. He parked, helped Ellie out, and grabbed their bags.

Keeping his hand on her elbow, he escorted her inside the reception area. "Evening, Ralph."

"Logan and…"

"Ellie," Logan answered.

"Ah yes. If you'll both sign in." Logan did and then he gestured to Ellie. She signed in, then Ralph held out a white wristband. When Ellie didn't move to take it, Logan did, then tugged her away from the desk.

"Didn't Max go over the sign-in procedures with you?"

"He did." Her cheeks and neck were flushed. "What is that for?" She gestured to the wristband.

"It's for you." He fastened it around her wrist. "It should have been explained when Max explained protocols."

"I don't remember anything about this." She turned her wrist one way and then the other.

"I'll explain after we change, but please don't remove it."

"Yes, boss." She gave him a small salute and disappeared into the women's room.

Logan laughed. Smarty pants. He made his way into the men's room. Luckily for him, he didn't have a lot of changing to do, but he suspected Ellie did.

* * * *

Ellie stared at herself in the full-length mirror. *Passable.* She had limited clothing for club attire, and she wasn't about to go nude. She found an old sports bra and a pair of shorts, since she didn't own boy shorts, at least not yet. She hoped they were okay. She was happy she actually remembered what Max told her about the lockers, so she was able to secure her purse and belongings. Now to walk out.

Sucking in a deep breath, she made her way out of the ladies' room. Logan was leaning against the wall, waiting. Her breath whooshed out of her. He was now bare chested, and… Damn, the man must work out. His chest was sculpted, and those wide shoulders were rippled with muscle.

Wow, just wow. Her gaze took in his black pants—they looked like cotton—and the loafers on his feet.

Her gaze slid up his body until she met his dark brown eyes. "Am I okay?"

"You're beautiful."

A tell-tale flush flowed over her body. How long had it been since she'd been with a man? Longer than she realized. She'd only dated a few times since her divorce and not much in the last five years. "Thank you." Where was her bold side? It wasn't like her to be this shy.

"Let's go." Logan cupped her elbow and led her to the double doors. He opened one.

Instantly, the music hit her. Some sort of hard rock? It had a consistent beat to it. Logan nudged her inside and shut the door behind them.

"Welcome to Wicked Sanctuary."

Ellie had been focused on the music, but now she saw the people. Her eyes went wide. Compared to when Sierra gave her a tour, the lights were lower, and of course now there were people in the club. Ellie took a deep breath and recognized body heat, sweat, and… She couldn't put her finger on it, but if sensuality had a smell, that would be it. "I…" She had no idea what she'd wanted to say.

"Let's go sit down." Logan led her to a set of sofas in a back corner. On the way, she saw men and women in all sorts of dress. Some like her, in bra and shorts, others just a thong, some with nothing. Ellie glanced down at her feet.

She wore modest one-inch heels, but others were in stilettos. How they walked in them, she didn't know. On any given day, she could barely handle the ones she had. Flats were her choice most of the time.

Logan gestured for her to sit and then sat next to her. "You're overwhelmed."

"A bit. Are my shoes okay?" She glanced over his shoulder and saw all sorts of stages with equipment on some of them. Ellie was sure she was going to get one heck of an education tonight. A shiver of excitement skimmed over her skin.

He glanced down at her feet. "They're fine. The shoe requirements have been changing over the last year."

"Oh?"

"Yes, Sierra and the other subs convinced Max to let them wear flats saying heels were too much and they weren't going barefoot."

Ellie shivered. "It might be unsanitary to go barefoot."

"The floor is sanitized nightly, but you might be right." Logan shifted. "Remember we talked about you calling me Sir in the club? I'm going to suspend those protocols with me tonight, but don't forget them with others." He rested against the back of the sofa and put his arm around her shoulders. "Close your eyes for me."

Ellie did as he said.

"Deep breath in and let it out just as slowly."

Again, she did as he said.

"Now, keep your eyes closed and listen. Besides the music, what do you hear?"

Ellie concentrated. "People talking, the snap of something, maybe a moan or something like that."

"Good. Now open your eyes."

She did, and Logan was leaning close. Ellie took a breath and inhaled his scent of leather and masculinity. Thank goodness he'd suspended the protocols, because she could barely think with him so close.

"Is there anything that is scaring you?"

Ellie tilted her head. "No, why would…" She stopped when she saw his face, then chuckled. "I don't know how you knew, but yes. At first glance, it overwhelmed me. But I hear no screams and no one's in pain that I can tell."

"Right. This isn't about pain; this is about pleasure." His breath brushed her skin. "If you see something you don't like, tell me. I'll explain it to you, but you don't have to watch."

She nodded. This wasn't what she'd expected. Or was it? Sierra and the others talked in generalizations about the club, but some of the books she'd read were more detailed, and some of them were wrong, it appeared. Pain and pleasure didn't have to go together.

"Now, the wristband." His fingers encircled her wrist. "You're wearing a white one; that means novice."

"Yours is blue."

"Blue signifies a Dom."

Ellie nodded.

"Once you've been in the club a while, you'll see all different ones. Yellow is a dungeon master, if you need help or are scared, go to one of them."

"Not my Dom?"

"Only if your Dom isn't available or you don't have one. While we're together, I'll be your Dom."

What would it be like to surrender to Logan? Intense would be one feeling, but she was sure there were more.

"Black is for a master, you'll see those on Max, Jordan, and Damon."

"What about the subs?"

"We talked about white, purple and white is a taken sub. Pink and white is a medium experienced sub. Green and white is experienced sub."

"I don't know if I'll remember all of them." That was a lot of colors and combinations.

"You really only need to remember the Doms, and if you see red or red and white, those are for Sadists and masochists."

"I'll make sure to stay clear." Those terms made her nervous.

"A Sadist could approach you, but remember you have the right to say no to anyone in the club."

"Including you?"

"Including me. Wicked Sanctuary is all about consent. Safe, Sane, and Consensual. If you don't believe in that, Max doesn't allow you membership."

"Okay, but how does Max know I'm a sub. I didn't put that on my application."

"I know." He stared at her. "Will you trust me on this?"

Ellie stared back at him. "You think I'm a sub?" Was she?

"I do. You might have some dominant traits, but I see that more in your business than I do in your sensual side."

In a way, that made sense to her. "Okay, I'm willing to give it a shot."

Logan grinned. "Good. Would you like to walk around or just sit here and take in the place?"

"If we could sit here a few more minutes, I have some questions."

Logan settled back on the sofa, and Ellie took a breath of relief. At least his breath was no longer caressing her skin nor his lips so close to hers. What was she thinking? He was only her mentor, not her lover or anything like that.

"Tell me about that area over there." She pointed past him to another sitting area.

"The sub area. That is where subs get together to sit or to talk or wait for their Doms or partners for the evening."

Ellie frowned. "I don't understand. They can't wander around the club?" That didn't seem fair.

"They can. It's up to them. Usually, a group of them will sit there and talk. Either way, Max wanted a space where they could gather, so he set this up." He glanced over. "Sierra and Tessa are there, which means Max and Damon are probably on duty. Emily and Harper are talking with them. They're unattached, so they're probably waiting to see if anyone approaches them."

"Not everyone is attached?"

"No, there are a lot of players who are single and enjoy the club, along with married couples."

"So, if you're single, you can play with whomever you want?"

"Yes. The sub has the right to say yes or no to any Dom."

"What about the married ones?'

"That's why we have the *taken* wristbands. Doms usually won't approach a taken sub, and if they do, they are expected to respect the band."

So much information. A shadow fell over them and Ellie looked up. Sage?

"Evening, Logan, Ellie," she said.

"Sage, it's good to see you here," Logan stood and waved her to sit, but Sage shook her head.

"Brady will be here any minute. I wanted to stop and say hi, especially since I found out Ellie joined." Sage looked at her, and Ellie's face heated. "I'm glad they didn't scare you at the bachelorette party."

Ellie's gaze moved to Sage's wrist. She wore a blue wristband. That's right, she was a Domme. "They are an intimidating bunch, Ma'am," Ellie said.

"They can be." Sage's gaze went to the front. "There's Brady. We'll come say hi later." Sage walked away. That's when Ellie noticed what she was wearing. A red and black corset with a black thong and sheer lace thigh-high stockings. The heels on her shoes were at least four inches, and she walked with confidence and swagger across the room.

"Wow, she looks…fantastic. Powerful," Ellie said.

"Sage is a Domme." He retook his seat next to Ellie.

"She told me."

"When?"

"At the bachelorette party. We were chatting."

Logan grinned. "That sounds like Sage. Brady is her sub."

"That's why she's wearing a blue wrist band. She's a Dominant."

"Yes. There are female Dominants, male Dominants, and then there are switches."

"I'm never going to understand all of this."

"You will. Switches swing both ways. Sometimes they're Dominants or Tops; other times, they're subs or bottoms."

"On my questionnaire, I wasn't sure what I was."

"Which is why we talked before coming to the club."

"And you figured out I was a sub from just talking with me?"

"Yes, but also in actions. You're independent and not about to let me order you around. Yet your demeanor softens when I'm near."

Ellie's breath caught in her throat. Damned if he wasn't right. There was an attraction between them, even if she didn't want it. But that didn't mean she would let it rule her life. She wanted to learn more about the lifestyle, and Logan was going to be a good teacher.

"You're way too observant."

"I was taught to be."

Another reminder of his job. Was she going to be able to deal with him being a cop? She reminded herself, again, it was only for the time of the classes. Once they were done, she could find someone with a safer occupation. A wave of sadness rolled over her at the thought of saying goodbye to Logan.

"I bet." She shifted on the sofa. "Can we walk around?"

"If you're ready." He stood and held his hand out to her.

Ellie put her hand in his, and tingles swept over her. She pushed them away. She would control her reactions to Logan. She had to. Her heart hung in the balance.

* * * *

Logan watched Ellie carefully as they talked. Her questions showed she had absorbed and thought about what he'd said and keenly observed the activity around them. He liked that about her. Ellie knowing Sage was a Domme surprised him. It shouldn't have. Sage wasn't one to keep it a secret, especially at something like Sierra's bachelorette party where almost all of the women were members of Wicked Sanctuary.

Finding a light flogging scene, he pulled Ellie to a halt and positioned her in front of him. "This would be a good one to watch." With her back against his chest, Logan could smell something tropical. Probably her shampoo. Citrus shouldn't be a turn-on, but damned if his dick didn't grow hard.

Oliver had Rose over a spanking horse and a light flogger in his hand. "This is Oliver and Rose. They've been together for a little while now."

"I've met Rose but not Oliver." Her voice was soft and low. "Except he was with you at the bachelorette party."

"He was. Keep your gaze on them. See him running his fingers over her skin." Logan wanted her to see the sensuality in the scene. Oliver leaned over and whispered something to Rose, and Logan heard a sigh.

"Is he talking to her?"

"Yes. While we can't hear what he's saying, it's common to make sure your sub is in the right headspace to play."

Ellie turned her head. "Headspace?"

"Like this." He slipped his arms around her waist. Ellie stiffened for a moment, then relaxed. "You stiffened when I put my arms around you, and it took you a second to get in the right headspace to relax."

"Interesting. I never thought about it like that."

"It's instinctive most of the time. When in a scene, I will make sure you're relaxed and ready before we do anything."

His arms felt good around her, especially when she relaxed against him. Oliver slapped Rose's ass several times then stopped, rubbing it and talking with her.

"What is he doing?" Ellie asked.

"He's making sure she's okay. It's important, especially while in a scene, to check in with your sub and make sure she's still green. You remember the club safe words, right?"

"Yes. Green is good. Yellow is slow down. Red is stop."

"Perfect. While we Doms try to read body language, it doesn't always work. We talk to our subs, and we expect them to talk to us. That way, you have control of how far you want to take things."

"That makes sense. And rubbing the sub's butt?"

"It helps with the sensation. Oliver is warming her up. You don't just start flogging someone. In order for both of you to get pleasure, the sub needs to be warmed up."

"I'm confused."

"Just watch. This is all new to you, and it will take time to process." Oliver had picked up one of the suede floggers. "There are different types of floggers depending on the experience of the sub."

"What would you use on me?" Her voice was soft, but her eyes stayed on the couple. Good. That's where he wanted them.

"I would start you off on a rabbit flogger. It's made out of rabbit fur, and you'd feel no pain, just a slight sting. Like fingers hitting your flesh."

"Like a spanking."

"Maybe a little bit harder." He decided to try something. "Hold your arm out, please." Ellie did as he asked, and he slapped her arm. "About like that."

"Ohh." She dropped her arm, but her breathing increased. Interesting. "And after that?"

"Depending, maybe half rabbit and suede. It's a mutual decision if and when we move to another flogger or not."

"So much communication."

"I believe that's why BDSM relationships last longer. Partners talk about everything. I'm not saying everyone is perfect; they're not. We do have some jerks."

"Really? Wouldn't Max sort them out."

"He does his best. But everything isn't caught by a background check or questionnaire." Logan kept his lips near her ear, enjoying the feel of Ellie in his arms. "Max, Jordan, and Damon make sure there is no funny business, and the subs are always welcome to tell them or any dungeon master, DM for short, if there's an issue."

"What if the problem is with a DM?"

"Max would have their ass. DMs are well vetted and have been with the club for a long time. Max takes the safety of his members seriously." Rose let out a small cry, and Ellie jumped. "Easy. What do you see?"

"She cried out, but she doesn't seem scared or hurt. She's smiling."

"Right. She's not crying in pain but because of the pleasure Oliver is giving her." He guided her away from the flogging scene and moved on to a bondage scene. They continued around the club for another hour before Logan took them back to the sofa.

Ellie's skin was flushed, her breathing rapid, her eyes wide. "Are you okay, Ellie?"

"Yes… No…" She blinked several times. "This wasn't what I was expecting."

"What were you expecting?" He wanted to know what she thought the club would be like.

"Darker. The club has good lighting. Women on their knees waiting for someone to pick them out. Less…I don't know…permission."

"Remember what I said about consent?" He wasn't surprised by her expectations. Many had misconceptions about the lifestyle.

"I do." She twisted her hands together in her lap. "Sage with Brady, they were…beautiful together."

They'd stopped to watch Sage tie Brady up and then torment him, but Ellie was right; it was beautiful. "Those two love each other." A true power exchange in his mind. He'd seen it many times with the committed couples in the club. Maybe one day he'd find the right woman. He looked at Ellie. Maybe he had. Only time would tell.

"One of the things I've noticed is that when partners trust each other to such a degree that control is surrendered from one to the other." He was surprised how easy it was to talk to Ellie. "The dominant partner is given, with fully informed consent, nearly complete control and responsibility over the submissive partner. To build such trust requires a degree of communication and give and take few relationships are able to achieve. There can be no secrets, no withholding."

"Is it the sub who always gives in?"

He shook his head. "No. It's about compromise, again, mutual give and take. Both parties give to each other and take from each other based on mutual agreement on what suits their dynamic the best."

"I think I get it."

"It's all in the partner negotiations."

"That all makes sense. I think." She yawned.

"And on that note, it's time to get you home." He stood and helped her to her feet.

"This has been wonderful, Logan. Thank you."

"Thursday night we'll be in the club again. But with fewer people here, you can explore more." He stopped in front of the ladies' room. "I'll be waiting for you when you come out."

She flashed him a grin and disappeared through the door. Logan made his way into the men's room with a lightness he hadn't felt inside him in a long time. He needed this. Wicked Sanctuary. Just being here tonight had helped him unwind. And Ellie.

Ellie was still a little bit of a puzzle to him. Maybe puzzle wasn't the right word. More of an exciting unknown he couldn't wait to dig into. But she seemed eager to learn about the lifestyle, and she'd listened and didn't jump to conclusions. He had a feeling this was a great start for the two of them.

Chapter 5

Ellie blew out a breath as she walked into Wicked Sanctuary with Logan on Thursday night. It had been a busy week, and she'd been looking forward to this. After Saturday night, she'd called Sierra Sunday and asked if she could buy Sierra lunch to talk.

Sierra told Ellie to meet her at Sweet & Savory at two and hung up before Ellie could remind Sierra it was Sunday, and the café was closed. When she arrived, Ellie was surprised to find Sierra and others at the café.

Once inside, Sierra explained that every Sunday, if needed, the subs of the club got together to chat. It helped not only the newer subs, but the older ones as well. Even Brady was there, and Ellie had a great time talking with everyone.

She learned a lot. They gave her a list of books to read, and Tessa told her to come to the bookstore attached to Kleinman's Monday evening, and she'd help her find everything.

Kleinman's was an adult store. Damon owned it. She shouldn't have been surprised after finding out about Damon's adult toy business at the bachelorette party, yet she was. But Tessa met Ellie at the bookstore and found everything Ellie wanted. Destiny, who managed the two stores, was a hoot. With purple hair, fishnet stockings, and a body Ellie envied, she kept Ellie laughing.

The adult store was nothing like Ellie thought it would be. She actually enjoyed herself and was pleased that the mask she wore was slowly coming off. She'd been on her own for a while and had built up some hefty protection. Sierra, Crystal, and Tessa had been getting behind her mask since day one, and Ellie was more than grateful.

She changed and wondered what Logan would think of her outfit. When she walked out of the ladies room, his eyes widened, and he grinned.

"Like?" she asked, holding her arms out and doing a little spin.

"Fucking gorgeous." His gaze went from her head to her toes. "I see you did some shopping."

"Yes, with Tessa's help." Ellie smoothed her hands down over the short black skirt. The black bra lifted her breasts, and the cute flat red shoes sealed the outfit.

"Remind me to thank her." Logan snagged her around the waist and led her inside the club.

"It's a lot less crowded tonight," Ellie commented. The music was still a techno beat, but not as loud as Saturday.

"Yes. Thursdays are for the classes or demos, depending on what is going on." Logan led her over to the sofas. They sat. "What would you like to do tonight?"

Ellie blinked in surprise. "You're asking me?"

"Yes." Logan grinned. "This is all for your learning pleasure, Ellie."

She glanced around the club. "Can we look at the equipment so I can understand more about it?"

"We can." He stood and held his hand out to her.

That was one thing Ellie noticed. Logan always helped her up, in and out of his vehicle, keeping a hand on her arm as they walked. He was protective, yet gentle. She hadn't had that in her life, not since her brother died.

"Where to first?" he asked.

Ellie looked around. "That." She pointed to the stage area that held an odd-looking chair.

"You got it." He guided her over and up onto the small stage. "This is a bondage chair. Have a seat."

She sat down on the hard wood. "Is this oak?"

"Teak." Logan said walking behind her. His hands settled on her shoulders, then slid down her arms. "While it may seem tame"—he lifted her right arm parallel to the wooden arm—"it's fun to use on a sub."

She turned her head and saw something in Logan's hand. "This is hemp rope. Meant to be soft and not scratch tender skin." He stroked her arm, then made a loop, slid it over her wrist, and tightened the loop.

The rope tickled her skin with its softness. She watched as he began winding the rope up her arm, pinning it against the wood. When he reached her shoulder, he stretched the rope around the back of the chair, to her other side, and began doing the same to her left arm.

When he got to her wrist, he tied off the rope. Then Logan ran his finger around the rope over both arms. She shivered with awareness at his touch. It was soft, yet firm. Like a caring Dom.

"Why are you doing that?"

"To make sure the rope isn't too tight against your skin."

"Don't you want it tight?"

"Enough to hold you yes, but not to cut off circulation or harm you." He stepped in front of her. "Wiggle your fingers." She did. "Good. Now how do you feel?"

Until he asked, she hadn't realized how vulnerable she felt. "A little vulnerable."

"Which is why you only play with someone you trust. Normally, I would have discussed this with you before we even started. Negotiations are part of the deal; remember that."

"Why didn't you?" He was right. She should have talked with him before they started. That she trusted Logan surprised her. Max was watching them, though he didn't join them. Was everyone and everything in this club designed to make subs feel safe?

"I wanted to see how you'd react." He knelt in front of her. "I would never do anything to hurt you. I trusted you to call your safe word if you were scared." He put his hands on her thighs.

"Yellow."

Logan froze, and Ellie took a deep breath. He stared up at her. "What is it?"

"What are you going to do?" She hated the tentativeness of her voice.

"Thank you for saying your safe word." Logan removed his hands. "Do you want me to undo your arms?"

"No." She swallowed. "But I'm not ready to go in blind. Tell me what you were planning to do."

Logan's eyebrows rose. "I forgot to remind you of the protocols in the club."

Her face heated. Damn, how could she have forgotten that? Easy, she hadn't been thinking but feeling. Her emotions overrode her brain. "I'm sorry, Sir. Would you please tell me what you were planning to do?"

"I am going to show you how the chair works."

"Can I ask that you talk me through this, Sir?"

Logan grinned. "Good idea." He shifted. "I'm going to place my hands on your thighs and push your legs apart."

This time his touch wasn't such a shock to her. He pushed her legs apart along with the legs of the chair.

"Oh my goodness." Her breath caught in her throat. Ellie had a pair of boy shorts on under the skirt, but she could just imagine if she was naked, how open she would be.

"Normally, I would restrain your legs as well, but not today."

As well? Ellie had forgotten her arms were tied up. How could she forget that? Maybe because her concentration was on Logan.

"Now, once I have you in the position I want you..." He reached underneath the chair, and she heard a click. "It's locked, and you wouldn't be able to close your legs if you were restrained."

"What would you do next, Sir?"

His dark brown eyes lit up. "Tease you."

"Tease me, how, Sir?"

"Shall I show you?"

She nodded before she even thought about it. Logan stood and motioned to Max, who sauntered over. "Would you grab my bag for me, please."

Max turned away and was back in a minute with a black bag. Logan took it from him and set it on the stage. He stood and took more rope from the table. "I'm going to tie your legs, calves and below."

"Okay, Sir." Her skin was already tingling and her nerves shimmering. While she still had that vulnerable feeling, there was curiosity that wasn't going away. This was what she'd come to Wicked Sanctuary to feel, to learn, and it excited her.

Logan tied her legs. She wiggled her toes but couldn't close her legs. Her heart rate picked up.

"I have you at my mercy," he whispered.

Damned if a thrill of anticipation didn't send her pulse skyrocketing as he unzipped his bag. She'd seen several of these Saturday night and had asked the girls about them. Toy bags, or Dom bags, as some called them.

Sierra said the Doms kept their personal equipment in them. Ellie was curious what Logan had in his, but he kept his body between the bag and her. When he straightened, he had a long black handle with a feather at the end of it.

"This is a feather tickler." Logan stepped up to her and ran it over the bare skin her bra didn't cover.

A quiver ran over her skin as he ran it over her stomach, down her legs, then over her arms.

"If you were naked, I'd use the feather to tease your nipples until they were hard peaks."

Just his words were making them hard, and she shifted in the chair.

"This is arousing you." Logan grinned at her.

"How do you know that, Sir?" Could he really tell?

"You shifted in your seat; your nipples are poking against your bra, and your breathing has gone shallow."

She hadn't even noticed her breathing. "Do you notice everything, Sir?"

"I try." He ran the feather from fingers to shoulder, then shoulder to finger. "How does this feel on your skin?"

"Soft, ticklish, Sir."

"Ready for something else?"

Ellie nodded, curious what he'd use next. Logan turned away. She kept her gaze on him as he knelt. She watched the muscles in his naked back and shoulders move as he dug around in his bag. Her gaze slid south. The black pants molded to his ass. What would it feel like to hold on to that ass as he plowed into her?

What the hell was she thinking? This wasn't about sex; it was about sensuality, about pleasure. Oh yeah, Logan would pleasure her all right. Ellie closed her eyes and tried to get her runaway thoughts in line. That didn't help. She could smell Logan. Leather and a hint of gun oil invaded her senses.

"Don't fall asleep on me," Logan said.

"Not a chance, Sir." She opened her eyes, but Logan was behind her again.

"I'm going to touch you, Ellie. Is that okay?"

Her pussy tightened, and she nodded.

"Words, please."

"Yes, please, touch me, Sir."

His palms rested on her shoulders, but they were covered in…fur? His fingers moved over her collar bone, and down. He toyed with the edge of her bra. Another shiver went through her body. The fur was soft against her skin, then a slight prickling feeling and back to soft. So confusing.

What she didn't expect was the sensation it evoked, as if his touch woke nerve endings she never knew she had. Anticipation hit her low in her belly. Would he dip beneath her bra?

No, he skimmed over the fabric, but when he got to her taut nipples, he paused. He tapped his palm lightly against her nipples, and she jerked in the chair. Oh dear God. How could she even explain the feelings tumbling on top of each other.

Pleasure, but so much more. She jerked at her arms, but they wouldn't move. How fair was this, that he could touch her, and she couldn't touch him. Before she could say anything, his palms slid over her stomach.

Ellie sucked in a breath.

"So beautiful," Logan whispered, still standing behind her. "How aroused are you, Ellie?"

"Very, Sir." She didn't know where the words came from.

He kept his palms on her abdomen. "Good. How else are you feeling?"

She wasn't sure what he was asking, but she didn't censor her words. "Vulnerable, aroused, confused, and downright frustrated, Sir."

He chuckled, and she wanted to smack him, but of course, she couldn't because she was tied up. Then his hands were gone. Instantly, she missed his caress.

"I think that's enough for tonight." Logan began to undo her arms, one at a time, massaging them as he removed the rope before gently lowering them to her lap. Then he undid her legs and fixed the chair so she was sitting normally once again.

Ellie tried to control her breathing, while also trying to understand what was going on. They were just getting started, and he called everything to a halt. Why?

Logan extended his hand to her, and Ellie allowed him to pull her out of the chair. Her legs wobbled, and instantly, Logan was there, his arm around her waist, holding her up. "I've got you." He guided her off the stage and into a new seating area.

Instead of letting her go, he maneuvered her around him, and the next thing she knew, he was sitting on the sofa with her in his lap.

She squirmed. "I'm much too heavy to be sitting in your lap, Sir."

"You're not." He tightened his hold on her waist. "Sit still. And you don't need to call me Sir now."

She stilled. His voice was low and hard. Had she done something wrong? She didn't think so.

"This is aftercare, Ellie."

"Aftercare?" She remembered something about that from her reading and the previous classes, but she didn't know it included sitting in his lap. "Why am I in your lap?"

"Because I want you there." He shifted, and she leaned against his shoulder. "Tell me how you feel about the scene we just had?"

"Is that what that was?"

"A modified one, but yes."

"It was fine. I was enjoying it until you stopped."

Another chuckle and Ellie wanted to smack him. "This isn't funny."

"How aroused were you?"

Her body heated. "Probably a five out of ten."

"Not bad for your first experience."

"Why did you stop?" She wanted to get to the bottom of that. Had she done something wrong? Enjoyed it too much?

"I didn't want to overwhelm you on your first time."

Ellie stared at Logan. "I wasn't overwhelmed."

"Oh?" His eyebrows rose. "I know you said your arousal was only a five out of ten, but how did your legs feel when you stood up."

"Like limp noodles." She wouldn't lie.

"Right. Your brain hadn't processed what your body was feeling, not yet. It was time to stop before you lost all thoughts and sank into the pleasure. Sitting here now, you can sort out everything that you felt."

Ellie considered his words. "Is sinking into pleasure and not thinking, something that happens often?"

"The more intense the scene, yes. But because this was your first time, everything was new and exciting. At least I think it was."

"It was different." She recalled the way the feather felt against her skin and then his hands. Interestingly, her body still tingled from his touch. "I think I get it."

"Good."

"Will you stop every time?"

"When I see you getting overwhelmed I will."

"But how did you even know?" She hadn't even realized she was that far gone.

"It's a Dom's trick of the trade." Ellie laughed, and Logan smiled. "That's my girl."

Heat flared deep within her at his words. Why did she suddenly want to be his girl? This wasn't like her. She pushed the words and feeling aside to analyze later.

"What now?" she asked.

"We sit here for a bit, then we can walk around some more, but no more play tonight."

She agreed with him. "Okay." Ellie yawned, laid her head against his shoulder, and closed her eyes.

* * * *

Logan enjoyed the feel of Ellie's body against his as she relaxed. She'd done great in the bondage chair. She hadn't panicked, and she'd used the safe word when she needed to. He hadn't been rushing her at all, but he was glad she made him slow down. It gave him an idea of what she was comfortable with.

She was very much a novice. Next week would be her last class, and he wasn't sure how he felt about that. If he didn't have to work this weekend, he'd suggest dinner. Maybe Wednesday night before their last class. It had to be her decision on whether they continued together after next week, or she struck out on her own.

Somehow, he thought she'd stick with him. He was safe. One brow rose as he gazed off into the distance, and a smile began slowly. Oh, the things she didn't know about him yet. If she wanted to continue with him in the club, they'd have some bigger conversations, but until then, he was content just being with her.

It was funny, in a way. He hadn't even kissed her, and she'd wormed her way beneath his skin. He'd kept his relationships pretty light due to his job. He didn't think it was fair to commit to one woman when his job was volatile. So many things could happen.

Even though Ellie had been surprised at his job, she hadn't mentioned it again, nor had she shied away from him. That was nice, and he hoped it meant they were past that. She stirred in his arms, and her eyes opened.

"Oh dear. I'm sorry."

"For what?" He turned his head and brushed his lips over her forehead.

Her eyes closed, then opened. "I think I was a little too relaxed."

"Everyone reacts differently after a scene, some are high with energy, others need to cuddle, and like you, some just need to be held to let their bodies relax."

"You don't mind?"

"No. I like holding you in my arms."

"I like being here." Her eyes grew wide when she realized what she said.

Logan let the comment pass. He didn't want to scare her off. "How are you feeling?"

"Good. Relaxed, like I've had a good massage."

"How did you feel about your first scene?"

Her nose scrunched up, and he was hard pressed not to kiss it.

"It was good, I think. Different."

"Did being bound bother you?"

"Not really. When it was just my arms, I was okay. But when you did my legs, I felt vulnerable and a little nervous."

He'd expected that. "You called out your safe word, which was exactly what you should do."

"Thank you. I was hesitant to do so."

Logan frowned. "Never be hesitant to call yellow or red if you need to or even if you're not sure."

"I appreciate you stopping."

"Any Dom worth anything would stop. You said yellow, so I was aware you weren't objecting to what I was doing but needed me to slow down. I should have talked to you more before we started."

"Don't blame yourself." Her voice was fierce. "I was excited to scene."

"You didn't know what to expect, and it's my responsibility to prepare you. I won't let it happen again."

"Logan." Her palm touched his cheek. "You did fine. I don't want you to take on the responsibility of my newness to the lifestyle."

"So sweet." He turned his head and kissed her palm. "I have to work this weekend, or I'd suggest coming back tomorrow night. But I would like to take you to dinner again. Are you available Wednesday night?"

"I am, and I'd like that."

"Good. It's almost eleven, and I know you have to work tomorrow."

"Eleven? How do you know that?"

"There's a clock behind the bar."

She sat up in his lap and looked toward the bar area. "I never noticed."

"Most don't. Max keeps it there because no phones are allowed, and some of the Doms don't wear watches in the club because they can catch on things."

"I noticed that most women don't have jewelry on."

"Right."

She squirmed.

"Ready to stand?"

"Yes, please."

Logan shifted her off his lap onto the sofa, stood, then helped her to her feet, keeping his hands on her waist.

"You do that a lot."

"What?"

"Keep your hands on me, be it to make sure I'm steady on my feet or to guide me when we're walking."

"Maybe I like touching you." Her cheeks bloomed, and Logan chuckled. "Let's go change, and I'll get you home."

"Bossy," she muttered as he guided her across the club.

"You have no idea."

Chapter 6

Saturday, Ellie unlocked the door of her business, Double Rainbow Party Planning. She loved the light that spilled into the main room from the windows. After making her way to her office, she sat at her desk and tucked her purse away. Her mind hadn't been on work the previous day. No, her mind was filled with Logan. Thursday night had been so different for her. Logan's touch sent her heart into overdrive, and even now, she swore the sensation of his skin sliding against hers echoed in her veins.

She'd slept like a log Thursday night, then last night, she had dreams about Logan and all the things he could do to her. When she woke, she was hot and aroused. Wednesday night seemed like a long time away, but he was working. She sighed. Cop. She had ignored what he did for a living, but she really couldn't continue to do that for much longer.

Going into this with her eyes open was the only way it could work. They needed to talk about his job, and she wanted to see if he wanted to continue in the club. She hadn't been sure of him at first, but the last two weeks had shown her he'd make a great partner in the club.

The bell over the door to her store jingled, and she walked out of her office to see her newest client walking through the door. "Good morning, Annette."

"Hi, Ellie." Her bubbly voice made Ellie grin. "I hope this is a good time."

"It's fine." Ellie pushed all thoughts of Logan out her head. Annette had come in a few weeks ago, asking if Ellie could do a divorce party. They'd talked, and Annette said she'd be back to talk logistics and timing.

"I probably should have called ahead." Annette examined several items in a basket of decorations. "I love these," Annette said, picking up the purple streamers and flowers.

"Come sit down, and we can talk colors for the party and other things." Ellie grabbed paper and pen from the table and pulled out a chair for Annette. Annette sat, and Ellie took a seat across from her.

Ellie found it easier to chat with the client that way. It also helped her get a feel for what the client wanted. "Let's talk decorations."

"I'm thinking the purple and yellow."

"Bold choices." Not two that Ellie would put together, but it was the client's party.

"I like purple and yellow. They remind me of spring, especially since we're going into fall."

"I can work with it." Ellie wrote on her check list Annette's choice. "Have you picked a venue yet?" She'd given Annette a list of places several weeks ago to check out. Ellie found it better if the client selected the venue.

"Yes, I've rented the banquet room at the Double D BBQ for Friday night, three weeks from yesterday."

"I can work with that." She made more notes. "How about—"

The front door to Ellie's shop was thrown open so hard, it ricocheted off the wall. Ellie jumped up.

Annette gasped, and all color drained from her face.

"You bitch," the man yelled.

Oh shit. Was this the ex? Ellie placed herself in front of Annette. "Sir, you need to leave." Ellie kept her tone firm and, at the same time, walked backward, pushing Annette toward her office.

"No way." He stood inside, legs wide apart, arms folded over his chest. He was a big man. Ellie swallowed. If he rushed them, he could catch them.

"I'm with a client right now. If you want to hire my party planning services, you need to make an appointment." Ellie kept walking backward a step at a time, her gaze never leaving the man. Good thing she knew how close she was to her office because she'd left her phone on her desk.

The intruder's voice boomed through the small space. "I don't need an appointment. Annette, get your ass over here."

"Not going to happen," Annette said, her voice unsteady.

The man's face flushed red, and he curled his hands into fists. *Oh this was so not good.* Ellie risked glancing over her shoulder. They were close enough, so she turned, pushed Annette into her office. Rushing in behind her, Ellie slammed the door and locked it. She heard a yell of outrage as footsteps sounded close to the door. Her heart pounded.

Annette ran to the far corner, looking like a deer caught in headlights. Ellie jumped when the man pounded the door.

"Open this fucking door." He continued his assault, the door reverberating with each strike.

Ellie took a deep breath, picked up her landline, and dialed 911.

"9-1-1, what is your emergency?"

"Ellie Tanner, seventeen thirty-two Jackson street. Double Rainbow Party Planning. I have an intruder in my shop, and he's belligerent."

"Police on the way. Is he armed?"

"I didn't see a weapon."

"Are you in a safe place?"

"For the moment." She was so glad she had reinforced her office door and walls. One could never be too safe when working alone. Plus, she never kept money in the store, which reduced the risk most of the time.

"Open up, you bitches. It's time to pay the price for your deceit, Annette."

"Where are you?" the operator asked.

"In my office. The door is reinforced. I'm here with a client."

"I've relayed the information to the officers, they should be there within a minute or two."

More pounding on the door and now he was kicking it. Ellie glanced at the bat she kept in her office for emergencies, hoping she'd never have to use it. She would never be a victim again, and she certainly wouldn't let her client be one. Ellie glanced at Annette.

Tears were running down her face. Ellie sighed. "It will be okay, Annette."

"He's my ex. I left him because he hit me. I thought having the divorce party would wash him away. I have a restraining order against him," Annette whispered. "This shouldn't be happening."

"Let the officers know my client, Annette Carpenter, has a restraining order against the man. He's her ex-husband."

"Letting them know. They are pulling up now. Hang tight."

Ellie waited.

"Pleasant Valley police. Sir, step away from the door." The officer's composed but firm voice calmed Ellie's nerves. The voice also sounded familiar.

"They're here." Ellie hung the phone up.

"You bitches called the police?" The door shook again. Annette whimpered.

Ellie drew Annette into her arms. "He can't get in." Ellie had made sure of that. She didn't care if the shop got wrecked; she and her clients were protected in this room. Well, as protected as they could be.

"Sir, back away from the door."

"Go to hell."

The next thing she heard was several thumps and then quiet. A knock on the door sounded loud. "Ma'am? It's the police. Mr. Carpenter has been detained. It's safe to open the door."

Ellie took a deep breath, released Annette, and unlocked the door. Bracing her body behind it, she opened it a crack. As soon as she saw Logan, it felt like her bones turned to noodles. She hadn't realized Logan was a patrol officer. Her body went limp.

His eyes widened when he saw her. "Ellie? Are you okay?"

She opened the door fully. "Now that you've restrained him." Ellie jerked her chin to where Annette's ex stood with two other offices in handcuffs.

"I'm just trying to talk to my wife," the man yelled.

"Ex-wife," Annette said, her voice shaking.

"By threatening these two women," one of the officers said.

"I didn't mean anything by it."

Ellie shivered. How many times had she heard that from her ex? She turned away from the door. "It's okay, Annette, the police are here."

"Thank goodness." Annette moved toward her. "This is the fifth time he's violated the restraining order."

"Officer Wolfe, ma'am." His eyes softened. "I'll need a statement from both of you." He glanced over his shoulder, and the other two officers took Annette's ex away.

Ellie stepped out of her office and looked around at the mess: Books and papers all over the place, chairs turned over, and it looked like there was crack in the wood frame of the front door. She sighed.

"It will be okay," Logan said softly.

"I'm not worried." She wasn't. All this was easily repairable, Annette's psyche was another thing. Logan grabbed a couple of chairs, straightened them, and gestured for them to sit.

Annette practically fell onto the chair. "I'm so sorry, Ellie. I had no idea he'd follow me here."

"Don't worry about it." Ellie patted Annette's hand. "This is an easy clean up." Wasn't that the truth? Blood was a lot harder to clean, right? She closed her eyes and took a deep breath, reminding herself that she was older and wiser now, and her safety plans had worked.

Logan took a seat across from them. "Please tell me what happened here."

* * * *

Logan watched Ellie's face. Rage flowed thought him, but he did his best to keep a lid on it. Ellie was very composed for someone who'd been confronted by a raging ex-husband. He wrote down Ellie's and Annette's statements. He offered Annette an escort home, but she refused.

He walked with Annette to her car then returned to Ellie's shop, where she was already picking up the mess. Her brunette hair floated around her shoulders, hiding her face.

"Are you okay?" he asked.

"Fine." She waved her hand in the air after she set books back on the table. "Good thing I don't have any other appointments today."

Logan stayed to take statements and because he needed to know Ellie was okay. "Does this happen often?" he asked as he straightened the chairs. How could a party planning business draw this kind of clientele?

"No, it doesn't." She blew out a breath but still wouldn't look at him. "You don't have to stay."

"I do." Logan noticed how she fluttered around, picking up and straightening things. Her hands shook, a telltale sign of stress. "Ellie," he said her name softly, and when she looked at him, he opened his arms. "Come here."

She all but ran into his arms. He pulled her into his embrace. "It's okay, sweetheart."

"I feel so bad for Annette," she whispered.

"Why?"

"Because he'll be out of jail by Monday. I wish we had better laws."

He did too. "Wait, how do you know he'll be out by Monday?"

"The DA won't want to prosecute, he'll be let go with a warning, not that it will do much good."

Logan frowned. "You seem to know a lot about this type of situation." Who had hurt her? Her ex? He wanted to punch something at the thought of violence touching her.

"I told you I was married. My ex was a bit of an ass. I had to get a restraining order."

"And he didn't obey it, did he?" Logan knew the answer. It wouldn't take much to search the database and get information on her ex and have a little man-to-scum chat with him.

She shook her head. "He thought he was clever and confronted me as I came out of a college class. Thankfully, other students thought he was acting strange and waited around. The second he hit me, they were on him. The cops were called, not that they did much."

"Ellie." His breath rushed out of him. Some man dared hit her. He cupped her cheeks with his palms. "I'm sorry that happened." Was that why she didn't care for cops? He knew some of his cop brothers didn't take domestic abuse as seriously as they should, and it made him angry. But he couldn't show that to Ellie. She deserved tenderness not rage.

"I never should have married him. Anyway, he was charged with assault and battery due to all the witnesses." She sighed. "He served only a year in jail. I wanted a longer term in jail, but the DA told me it was the best they could do. I was glad he left the state after his release. Last I heard, he's serving time somewhere in Colorado. He's out of my life."

"I'm so proud of you for staying calm." He looked around. "There's no one else with you here in the shop?"

"No. I'm used to working alone."

"It's not safe." He hated this. He'd ask central to have a patrol car come around every hour to make sure she was safe. Hell, he'd do it himself.

"I'll admit this isn't the first time I've dealt with an outraged ex-husband or wife, disgruntled mothers, fathers, or heck, even bridezillas. It's part of the business."

He really hadn't expected this from a benign business like hers. Logically, Logan knew she was right about being safe, but his gut said *protect*. He opened his mouth, and she placed her now steady fingers against his lips.

"I do everything to protect myself. My office is reinforced. The door has steel in it. You can't kick it in.

"You can if the hinges give out."

Ellie shook her head. "Reinforced hinges and door jamb. It's darn near a panic room. Also I have no money on the premises." She sighed. "Irritated clients are part of the job, but I'm a realist and prepared."

"This guy wasn't a client."

"Yeah." She blew out a breath. "Logan, really, it's okay." She stepped out of his embrace.

"I don't like it." He crossed his arms over his chest.

"You don't have to. Now go back to work. Please. I'll finish cleaning up here and then close early for the day."

Logan was about to argue when his radio went off. Damn. "Officer Wolfe, I'm on it." A disturbance in the park. "Be safe." He stared at her. "I did give you my phone number, didn't I?"

"Yes."

"Call me if you get scared, need help, or just to talk."

"I will."

His radio went off again.

"Go." She shooed him with her hands.

He turned and left her, but as soon as this call was done, he'd circle back to check on her.

* * * *

Ellie locked the door after Logan left, then sighed. What a day, and it wasn't even noon. Her heart rate had finally settled down. She finished cleaning up the shop, then went into her office. There was no way she could concentrate on anything after what happened. Too many memories.

She picked up her cell phone and stared at it before she dialed. "Hey, Sierra, it's Ellie."

"What's up?"

"I was wondering if you're free for lunch?"

"Sure, I'm meeting Crystal and Tessa at Sweet & Savory at one. Why don't you join us?"

"That would be great." Ellie needed to get out of her head, and she trusted these women. "See you there. And…thank you."

Forty-five minutes later, Ellie walked into Sweet & Savory. She loved Lara's place. The café was bustling, like always, but Lara saw her and waved her over. "By yourself?"

"No. I'm meeting Sierra, Crystal and Tessa for lunch."

"I've already got a table reserved in the other room. Do you want to order?"

"I can wait in line, Lara." The line had at least ten people in it.

"Even if I say you don't have to?" Lara smiled.

"Yes." Ellie turned and took her place at the end of the line.

The line moved quickly, and Ellie placed her order, then Lara showed her to the table. She'd just sat down when Sierra, Crystal, and Tessa arrived.

"Ellie," Sierra said.

Ellie stood and gave her a hug. "Sierra." She looked at the other two. "Crystal, Tessa."

"Don't think you can get away without hugging us too," Crystal said.

Ellie laughed and hugged both women. Crystal and Tessa sat.

"I'm off to order our food. Ellie, it looks like you ordered already?" Sierra said pointing to the number sitting on the table.

"I did."

Sierra walked away.

"So how are you two?" Ellie asked. While she'd seen the two women around the club, they hadn't talked much.

"I'm good," Tessa said.

"Tired, but good," Crystal commented. "I'm glad you could come to lunch with us."

"I feel like I'm crashing. I called Sierra, and she invited me."

"You're not." Tessa glanced around the café. "It's good to talk outside the club and the sub meetings if you need to."

Sierra sat down and plunked her number on the table. "It's going to be a little bit. Lara said they got backed up." Sierra looked at Ellie. "I'm glad you called me. Is everything all right?"

"I am too." Ellie looked at the hands resting in her lap, unsure how to start the conversation. "I need to discuss something that happened today."

All three women sat up straighter. "Did Logan do something?" Sierra asked.

"No. Logan was perfect, though a little overprotective. The ex-husband of a client came into the shop and threatened her."

"Oh no." Tessa squeezed Ellie's arm. "Is she okay?"

"Are you okay?" Crystal asked.

"We're both fine." Ellie's voice shook. Well, maybe she wasn't as fine as she'd like to think. "I just needed to talk this out with someone, and I don't have many friends."

"You do now." Sierra looked around the table.

"Thank you." It was true. While Ellie had grown up close to Pleasant Valley, she didn't have many friends in town, and those from her younger days had drifted away after she moved here. Not that she regretted it. Nope.

"So the ex came in…" Crystal prompted.

Ellie told them what happened, leaving nothing out, including that Logan was one of the responding officers, and how he'd stayed after her client left to help clean up before he got called away.

"Why do I think there's more to this story?" Tessa commented.

Ellie blew out a breath. "My ex abused me." The words came out without conscious effort.

"Fucker," Sierra said.

Ellie blinked. She hadn't heard Sierra swear before, at least not like that.

Crystal and Tessa laughed. "You should see your face," Tessa said.

"I bet." Ellie laughed.

"Do you want to talk about it?" Crystal asked.

"I think I do. I need this for myself, but also because I want to tell someone." She'd kept this bottled up for way too long. "I was eighteen and too young to know what I wanted in life."

"You must have loved him," Tessa said.

"Maybe. I'm not so sure I was ever in love with Gary. I think I was in love with the idea of having a place and someone to call mine." God, she sounded pathetic.

The women nodded. "Bad home life?" Crystal asked.

"Not really. Well, it wasn't exactly stable. My parents were on the third marriage each, and…" Ellie swallowed. Even after all this time, it was still hard to talk about her brother. "My brother had just died."

"Oh, Ellie." Instantly, she was swamped with warmth from these women. Her friends. Ellie blinked away her tears.

"Tommy was ten years older than me, but he was the best big brother." The memory of his dark wavy hair and blue eyes made her smile. "My parents seemed to move on after his death, but I was already floundering from being shuttled between them." Ellie took a deep breath. "He was a police officer."

"You said he died… Oh shit," Crystal said.

"While he didn't die on duty, he was shot while trying to stop a robbery at a convenience store he happened to be in." Ellie blinked, trying to stop the tears.

"That's horrible," Sierra said.

"Logan is a police officer," Tessa said softly.

"He is, and I had to think long and hard about that. However, he's just my mentor," Ellie said. She was bluffing, because she already knew she wanted more.

"Are you sure? I saw that scene Thursday night," Crystal said.

"That's all it can be. I can't fall for a cop. I can't." *Keep telling yourself that.* The truth was, she was already. There was something about Logan's protectiveness she liked. But it was more than that. Logan had found the hidden piece of her and brought it out in a way that no other man had, and he was patient and caring.

"We all think things can't go any further than the club," Sierra said, then glanced up as their food arrived. The women fell silent as they ate.

"How long were you married?" Sierra asked after a few minutes.

"Three years." Ellie shook her head. "I should have left him before the first year was out, but I stayed. I'm not sure why."

"Because we feel like failures, that it's our fault it isn't working out, and it's up to us to fix it," Crystal said.

Ellie's mouth dropped open. "How?"

"I've been there," Crystal answered.

"In some way, shape, or form, we've all been there," Tessa said.

"Mine was a verbally abusive ex-boyfriend and father," Sierra said.

"Mine was a religious family who thought they knew what was best for me," Crystal commented.

"Mine was a father and brother who thought they could control my life." Tessa shook her head. "Last year, my father threatened to expose Wicked Sanctuary. Thankfully, the town turned out to support Damon and the club."

"I remember that. I saw it on TV." That was how she became aware of Wicked Sanctuary, but she'd never really thought about becoming a member until she met Sierra.

"The thing is, a lot of women have trauma in their past, but we grow from it. I don't see you as a weak woman, Ellie," Sierra said.

Crystal laughed. "If she was weak, she would have run after seeing the Doms at your bachelorette party, Sierra."

Ellie laughed. "They were a bit intimidating."

"Crystal and I never thought they'd blame you for our decision, Ellie. We were the ones who picked the venue," Tessa said.

"You defended me. And all is good. The wedding and reception came off without a hitch, so I call it a win."

"And Logan drove you home after the bachelorette party," Sierra said.

"He did." Ellie thought back to that night. Was that when the attraction started? Probably. Logan was a sexy man.

"Don't let his job get to you, Ellie," Tessa said.

"I've known Logan for almost two years now, and he's a good guy," Sierra said.

"He is," Crystal agreed.

Ellie nodded. "I appreciate everything you've said."

"Are you coming to the club tonight?" Tessa asked.

"No. Logan is working, and I'm not out of my training yet."

"I can ask Max to make an exception," Sierra said.

"No, thank you. I'm good to wait. Besides, you ladies have given me a lot to think about." They had.

"I'm glad we could help. Now let's talk about our next party at the club," Sierra said.

"Are we talking a Halloween party or something else?" Tessa asked.

"Of course, Halloween. It will be two years since I met Max on that fateful night," Sierra said.

"How did you meet him?" Ellie asked. She couldn't see Max at a Halloween party.

Sierra laughed. "My ex-boyfriend took me to a horror camp, and I hate horror. So, I walked away from the campground and found myself caught in a storm and in front of the club."

"How? There's so much security."

"This happened before Max beefed all that up. Well, he did have the gate but apparently it had malfunctioned that night. I just thought he was having a party at his house when I knocked on the door. Imagine my surprise when he opened the door, wearing black pants, loafers, devil's horns, and nothing else."

Ellie's eyes widened. "Oh my God, I can actually see that."

"I'd like to make this Halloween special since we've been so busy."

Ellie thought for a moment. "What if we decorate the club. You could have fake spider webs everywhere. Maybe keep certain places a little dark, and we could have people jump out dressed in costumes."

"A costume party," Tessa said, clapping with excitement.

"Do you really think the guys are going to dress in costumes?" Crystal asked.

"Probably not," Sierra said. "The guys usually only wear masks or occasional horns or something on their heads. But that doesn't mean we can't decorate and have some fun."

"How much fun?" Ellie asked, her mind turning over the idea.

"We'd keep it to a members only party and limit how many people could come," Crystal said.

"What are you thinking, Ellie?" Sierra asked.

"I know someone who deals with Halloween parties, mainly for kids, but I bet I could borrow a few things from him."

"Like?" Tessa leaned forward.

"A big Frankenstein type mannequin where you can sit in his lap and have your picture taken. Dracula coming out of a coffin as you walk by. A couple of cackling witch boxes, stuff like that."

"That would be so much fun. What do you think about surprising the guys?" Tessa asked.

"That is brilliant," Crystal commented.

Sierra glanced at the calendar on her phone. "Halloween isn't until the end of next month, so we have a little over six weeks, and luckily, it is on a Saturday night. I might be able to convince Max to let us decorate."

"Won't he be suspicious?" Ellie asked.

"Of course, but he'll be good if I ask him nicely." A rosy tint touched Sierra's cheeks. Asking nice meant a lot more in a relationship.

Ellie wondered if she'd ever have something like that.

"I say let's do it," Crystal said.

"I agree," Tessa chimed in.

"And what are we doing?" Lara asked coming up to the table.

"Lara, perfect timing," Sierra said. "Halloween party at the club, Ellie is going to plan it, but would you do the food? And we're keeping the guys in the dark."

"Oh, this should be fun. I can do the food." Lara tapped her finger against her lips. "Can we get some fake male strippers."

The women burst out laughing. "That would give the guys fits."

"Oh my god," Ellie said trying to control her laughter. "Let me make some calls and see what I can do." She had contacts from other bachelorette parties.

"They'd go crazy, and they'd know it was us," Crystal said.

"They would, but think about how much fun the punishment would be," Lara said.

"Punishment?" Ellie's laughter died.

"She doesn't mean actual punishment, more like sexual punishment. Things like spanking, overwhelming you with a need to climax and not letting you, that kind of thing." A gleam sparkled in Crystal's eyes. "Trust me, with the right partner, it is so worth it. I was lucky I could walk the next day after the bachelorette party."

"Hell, I could barely sit down," Tessa said.

Ellie looked at her hands as her face heated. "Oh goodness, I never thought about that." She had so much to learn.

"We'll have to talk with the other subs and get buy-in from them, but I think we have another party to plan together ladies," Sierra said.

An hour later, Ellie left the café, feeling better than she had in a long time, and not because of the Halloween party. She finally had some good friends, and she was happy. Making her way to her car, she pulled out her keys and her cell.

Inside her car, she dialed Logan's number. It went to voice mail. "Hi, Logan, it's Ellie. I know you're working, but you have to eat dinner, right? Would you be interested in coming by my place for dinner tonight? Let me know."

After she hung up, she wondered if she'd done the right thing. Yes, she wanted to explore with Logan. She'd find a way to deal with his job. Or at least control her fear. She also had friends to talk her off the ledge if need be.

* * * *

Logan grinned when he listened to Ellie's message. When it finished playing, he called her back.

"Hi, Logan," she answered.

"Hi. I would love to have dinner with you tonight. What time?"

"Great. What time do you get off work?"

"I should be done by seven, but if an emergency comes up, it could be later." He sucked in a breath when she didn't answer right away.

"I can work with that. Why don't you text me when you get off."

"Are you sure?" Most of the women he dated didn't like how his job interfered with their personal and dating life.

"Yes. It's Saturday night, so I don't have to work tomorrow."

Logan's heart swelled. "I'll do that, but if it gets too late, I don't want you to think you have to do this. Or wait to eat your own dinner."

"Just text me. Be safe."

The line went dead, and Logan made no effort to stop the grin that crossed his lips.

"Hey, Wolfe, the chief wants to see you," one of the other officers yelled.

Logan raised his hand in acknowledgement, put his cell away, and headed for the chief's office, wondering what he wanted. But nothing could dampen his mood right now.

* * * *

Logan rang the bell for Ellie's apartment at seven forty-five. He'd been lucky and got off on time, ran home, showered, changed, and got to her place in record time.

"Yes." Ellie's voice came through the speaker box.

"It's Logan."

"Come on up." The door buzzed. He opened it and then made sure it closed securely behind him before going to the elevator. Ellie was waiting for him with her apartment door open.

"I'm glad you got off on time." She gestured for him to enter her apartment.

"Me too." He liked her place. Sometimes he thought that he should have stayed in an apartment instead of buying a house, but on his days off, he enjoyed doing yard work and lying in the hammock in his backyard.

"When you texted, I waited fifteen minutes to put the casserole in the oven, so it's going to be another five minutes." She gestured to the sofa. "Have a seat. What would you like to drink? I have water, soda, beer, and wine."

"A beer would be nice."

"Coming right up."

Logan glanced around the room. It wasn't like he hadn't been in her apartment before, but now he had time to study it. A good-sized TV on a stand across the room, a small DVD player, DVDs, and two bookcases full of books.

He grinned. Ellie like to read, and from what he could see from the sofa, romance and fantasy. He looked carefully at the romance books and saw some titles that were carried in Damon's store. Interesting choices. He turned his head as she walked back in with his beer in a mug.

"Here you go." She handed him the mug then took a seat in the overstuffed chair. Ellie tangled her fingers together.

Was she nervous? Upset? He didn't think so, but there was something on her mind. Was it what happened today? He sipped his beer, then set it on the coaster on the side table.

"You're looking nervous; what is it?"

"I do?" Her hand fluttered to her lips, then dropped. "I guess I am."

"I can leave if that would help."

"No." Ellie shifted in her seat.

"Is it about what happened today?" While she seemed to handle everything at the time, sometimes, once the event was over, reality set in.

"Partially."

"I can tell you the ex was booked. His arraignment won't be until Monday, so he'll spend the weekend in jail."

Ellie nodded. "Odds are the judge will let him go."

Logan stiffened. She was right. He hated it, but the guy's release was likely. "I'm sorry you have to deal with this."

"Not your fault. Unfortunately, the laws we have don't treat restraining order violations or domestic violence the way they should."

"I agree. But this time, he threatened another person, not just his ex. The judge will take that into consideration."

She nodded, but he saw something flash in her eyes. Her ex had hurt her, but how much? His muscles tightened. Logan knew he would defend Ellie from any danger. Always. "How can I help you?" he asked softly.

She looked at her hands in her lap. "There really isn't much you can do."

Damn. Today must have brought up memories she couldn't control. Did that mean she was going to tell him she couldn't finish out her mentorship with him? His chest hurt. How would this affect them at the club? He needed to get her talking. Maybe taking a different tack would help. "We haven't talked too much about triggers."

"Triggers?" Her voice was soft.

"Yes. Something I might do in play that will bring back a bad memory or cause you to panic."

"I hadn't thought about that. I don't know if I have any."

"Please come sit with me." He patted the cushion next to him.

Ellie stood as the oven timer went off. "Dinner," she said.

"Can you put it on warm, I'd really rather talk this out before dinner." He kept his voice soft to avoid making her feel like he was ordering her to do anything and dinner talk could be more relaxed.

"All right." She walked slowly into the kitchen, and it took her a few minutes to return. This time, she sat on the sofa and curled her legs under her so she faced him.

"You told me you were eighteen when you married and twenty-one when you got a divorce."

"That's right."

"How did your parents take it?" He was curious because she'd mentioned her parents' lifestyle choices.

"They just smiled and said these things happened. By the time my divorce went through, Mom was on her fourth marriage and Dad on his fifth."

Logan whistled. If he'd known her then, she wouldn't have had to worry about marrying the ass who hurt her. He would've made sure she was taken care of and safe. "That must have been rough." He had lost his father, but he was always sure of his parents' love and devotion to each other and to their children.

"It was, but…" She bit her lower lip. "A few days after I turned eighteen, my brother was killed."

"Fuck." Instinct told him they were about to get to the root of her feelings. Logan slid over and pulled her against him. "I'm so sorry, Ellie."

"I was too. He was my rock. After his death, my world didn't seem right."

"And then you got married?" He could almost see it in his head. Ellie lost without her brother. Her parents were too occupied with their grief to see what it was doing to her.

"Yes."

"I'm glad you found the strength to get out of the relationship. That couldn't have been easy."

"Life isn't easy." She took a deep breath.

"No, it isn't." He thought about the things he saw in his job.

"It took me a few years to realize that I was a better person than Gary tried to convince me of. I learned to be my own person, and I will never give that up again."

"You are a very beautiful person." He brushed his lips across her forehead. "If I ever do something that scares you, tell me."

"I will. So far, we've been good together."

"Yes." Then he remembered how they met. "You weren't intimidated by all of us the night of Sierra's bachelorette party." He recalled how she stood up for herself.

"I'm a strong woman, but yes, you guys were intimidating. I mean seriously; I turn and see a wall of tall, muscular men, standing shoulder to shoulder with their arms crossed over their chests." A tremor went through her body. "All that testosterone."

Logan laughed. "We are men, after all."

"I wanted you to know about my past before Thursday."

"I'm grateful and honored that you told me, but I do have to ask: What prompted you?" He was curious why she felt she needed to confess to him. Admittedly, he wanted them to go beyond Thursday night, but he hadn't approached her about it.

"Because I wanted you to know. And…um, I'm thinking maybe we could continue to be partners in the club after Thursday night."

Did that mean she didn't want to see him outside the club? If that was the case, why did she invite him over for dinner tonight? Now wasn't the time to analyze it. One step at a time.

"I'd like that." He wasn't going to turn her down. Once they played together a few times, he'd win her over to seeing him outside the club.

Ellie let out a breath. "Great. We should eat or the casserole will dry out." She slipped out of his embrace and stood. "I'm really glad you're here, Logan."

"So am I."

* * * *

They ate dinner and talked about their favorite books, TV shows, and movies. "I can't believe you still have a DVD player and DVDs," he said.

"I do stream, but some of the older movies I like aren't always available." They sat on the sofa again, this time with coffee.

"Makes sense." He finished off his coffee. It was getting late, and while she didn't have to work tomorrow, he did. "I should go." He set his mug down and stood.

Ellie stood and looked at her watch. "Oh goodness, I didn't realize it was so late. You have to work tomorrow, right?"

"It's fine." He took her hand in his. "I've had a wonderful evening."

"Me too." She looked up at him.

Logan took a breath. "I'm going to kiss you; is that okay?"

"Yes, please."

Logan lowered his head and brushed his lips over Ellie's. When he started to raise his head, her arms entwined around his neck, pulling his lips back down to hers.

Her tongue darted out and traced his lips, and Logan opened his mouth to her. Their tongues played with each other. He'd been trying to keep the kiss light, but damned if this woman hadn't taken the lead. And he didn't mind.

His arms tightened around her waist, pulling her up against him as he pushed his tongue into her mouth, tasting the coffee. Hell, he was drunk on her. Her kisses were sweet, sexy, and consuming.

He wanted nothing more than to pick her up and carry her into her bedroom, but it wasn't the right time. They were still getting to know each other. Logan pulled back. He rested his forehead against hers. "Damn, you kiss well. Thank you for dinner."

"My pleasure." Her voice was breathy, proving that kiss had affected her as much as it had him.

With effort, he disentangled himself from her embrace and opened the front door. "Lock it after me," he said.

"I will."

Logan stepped out and turned back. "I'm off Wednesday through Sunday, dinner on Wednesday?"

"I'd like that."

"Goodnight, Ellie." Logan couldn't help himself, he leaned down and brushed another kiss over her lips, then turned to leave. Ellie stood there. "Close door and lock it."

"Bossy," she muttered but did as he said.

Whistling as he walked to his vehicle, Logan decided maybe this mentorship was just what he needed.

* * * *

Ellie leaned against her apartment door. They kissed. Her fingers touched her tingling lips, and she closed her eyes. She had no idea how to describe the feelings flowing through her. Logan had been gentle at first, but when she took control of the kiss, it was like a switch flipped. And she hadn't minded at all.

In a daze, she pushed away from the door, cleaned up the kitchen and flopped down on the sofa. There was no way she could sleep now. Not with Logan running through her head. She picked up the remote and turned on the TV, found a romantic comedy she'd seen several times, and settled in to watch it.

He'd kissed her, and she couldn't wait until they kissed again. Thursday couldn't come fast enough.

Chapter 7

Thursday night, Ellie changed in the women's room of Wicked Sanctuary. Technically, it was her last class with Logan. She was glad there weren't a lot of people in the club; she was still a little self-conscious about all the skin she was baring in boy shorts and a bra.

She couldn't help herself. After the years of verbal abuse, she still didn't believe her body was worthy of someone like Logan. Sometimes she worried that maybe her ex was right. Was she too fat? Was her skin too pale? Did her thighs touch when she walked?

Ugh. Slapping the locker door, she pressed her thumb to the scanner and, hearing the click, turned and left the room. Her ex was her past, not her present, and that's all there was to it.

"Hey." A hand caught her elbow.

Instinct kicked in; Ellie turned with her arm already swinging.

"Woah, sweetheart." Logan captured her wrist in his hand.

"Logan." She blinked. "Sorry, you startled me."

"I see that and applaud your response. What would you do next?"

"What?" Ellie stared at him. What was he talking about?

"If a man captured your arm before you could hit him, what is your next move?"

"Are you serious?"

"I am. Next move?"

Ellie studied how Logan held himself. While he might look relaxed to some, she could feel the tenseness of his muscles, preparing for whatever might happen. "Well, I can't overpower you, so my next move would be to—" She brought her knee up, but stopped short of his groin.

"Nice move." His fingers gentled on her wrist. "I'm glad you can defend yourself."

"That's only one move. I know more." She'd taken self-defense classes several years ago.

"Good to know." He entwined his fingers with hers, and they walked into the club. Logan didn't stop until they were in front of a set of sofas. "Have a seat. We need to negotiate tonight."

"Okay, Sir." She complied and turned toward him as he sat.

"You remembered the protocols. Good job. I read over your questionnaire and your limits again."

"Again, Sir?"

"Yes. I read them before I became your mentor."

Ellie nodded.

"Max wouldn't have matched us if we weren't compatible, but I wanted to make sure there were no red flags."

"Like what, Sir?" Ellie frowned.

"Things like, if you liked pain more than I would be willing to give."

"Heck no, Sir."

Logan chuckled. "I know. You're looking for pleasure, and that's what I intend to give you. I'm not saying there won't be a little bit of pain. The bite of my hand spanking you can sting."

She smiled, and her body heated. "I think I can handle it, Sir."

"Your reaction when I surprised you just now tells me you'll let me know if you can't." He ran his finger over her cheek. "Since tonight is officially our last night as mentor and student, I want to push you a little bit."

"What do you mean by that, Sir?" Ellie kept her gaze on Logan.

"I want to tie you up in the bondage chair again, but this time, full restraints before I start touching you."

Ellie thought for a minute. "That's acceptable, Sir."

"I want to qualify what I mean by touching you; it will be over and under what you're wearing."

Her breath caught in her throat, and she swallowed. "Yes, Sir." Her voice was soft, but her nerves tingled with excitement.

"I want to be perfectly clear. I will be touching your breasts and nipples, and I will caress your pussy."

Color flooded her cheeks at his words. "Yes, Sir. I understand."

Logan nodded. "I'll be using the feather again and maybe a toy or two."

"Toy, Sir?"

"Nothing big, just something to enhance your pleasure."

"All right, Sir." Ellie wasn't sure what he could do while she was wearing clothing, but she was willing to try.

"The last thing is this: Are you okay being blindfolded?"

Ellie's eyes widened. "Blindfolded, Sir?" She hadn't thought about that. But she hadn't objected to it on her questionnaire.

"It will enhance your experience."

She thought for a moment and nodded.

"Words, please."

"Yes, Sir. I'm okay with being blindfolded."

Logan grinned. "Safe words apply as always. If you become uncomfortable or scared, use them."

"I'll do that, Sir."

"Good. Now our scene time is at ten-thirty. Shall we walk around until then?"

"Yes, Sir." Ellie swallowed. They'd gotten here at seven-thirty. It was probably close to eight-thirty, so two hours. The suspense was going to kill her.

* * * *

Logan kept an eye on Ellie as they walked. Their talk had gone well, but he wondered if she was still apprehensive about playing. He understood she wasn't quite comfortable with taking her clothes off. He could work with that, but tonight, he wanted to show her pleasure from his touch.

He'd planned this all out in his head. Restrain her in the bondage chair, blindfold her, use the feather tickler against her exposed skin, and with his fingers, he'd play with her breasts and nipples until she was squirming in the chair. Then he'd move to her pussy. He already had a couple of toys in his bag he could use even with her clothing on.

As it got closer to ten-thirty, Ellie shifted more and more from one foot to the other. Logan guided her across the club to a quiet area. He backed her up against the wall.

"Logan?" There was a slight tremor in her voice.

He didn't correct her for not saying sir. Sometimes you had to let protocols go. At least he felt that way. "You're nervous." He stroked her cheek, enjoying her smooth skin.

"A little, Sir."

His lips twitched as she remembered. "Safe words are always important."

"Yes, Sir."

Logan lifted her chin with two fingers until he could see into her eyes. "Is this going to be too much, Ellie?"

She blinked. "I…" Her lashes fell as her breathing accelerated.

He waited until she opened her eyes. "Answer me with total honesty. Do you want to scene tonight?"

Her eyes brightened as she answered. "Oh, yes, Sir. I guess I'm a little unsure about everyone watching."

Logan dipped his head until his lips were close to hers. "All they'll see is the beautiful woman I'm with." He brushed his lips over hers.

She inhaled, then her arms wound around his neck as she parted her lips in response to his silent invitation.

Logan didn't hesitate. His arms encircled her waist, pulling her flush against him as his tongue delved into her mouth. He could taste her unique flavor. He wanted more.

Soon, their tongues were tangling and doing their own little dance. Ellie moaned, and he took it as a sign to continue. He caressed the skin of her back, moving slowly downward until he found the band of her boy shorts.

Without hesitation, he slipped his hand beneath the fabric and cupped her ass. Another moan and she wiggled in his hold. Logan broke the kiss and stared down at her.

Her eyes were dreamy, her lips rosy red, and her skin flushed. "Your ass feels so good under my hand."

"Logan…Sir."

"Think about how you're going to feel as I play with your tits and nipples. When I plunge two fingers into your wet pussy and tease your clit with my thumb."

Thank goodness he was holding on to her, because her full weight pressed against him as if her legs had given out on her.

"I want that too." Her voice was soft.

"Then I shall give you what you want." He held her against him for several minutes until she could stand on her own. Logan slid his hand out from under her clothing and back to her waist. "Better?"

"Not as nervous, Sir," she said.

"Good, because it's time." Without giving her a chance to say anything more, he took her hand and led her over to the bondage chair. "Be right back." Logan left her standing there as he grabbed his bag from the cubbies next to the bar and returned. He took her hand and helped her up onto the stage and guided her over to the chair.

"Now remember: This is about pleasure. You start having any issues, arms go numb, you don't like what I'm doing, you feel scared, anything, use your safe words."

"Yes, Sir." The need and desire in her eyes almost brought Logan to his knees.

Reaching into his bag, he pulled out several lengths of rope. "Raise your right arm." Ellie did as he asked. Logan started by making a loop and putting it around her wrist and the wood of the crossbar of the chair, then he wound the rope around her arm.

He made sure to avoid her shoulder and neck area, then started down her left arm while she held it in place. Logan ran his fingers under the rope, making sure it wasn't too tight. "How are you doing?"

"Green, Sir." He expected that answer at this point.

Moving to her feet, he began to wind the rope from her ankles up her legs until he reached her thighs. Once both legs were restrained, Logan reached beneath the chair and pulled the pin loose.

Ellie took a deep breath as he pushed her legs apart and then replaced the pin. "Still green?"

"Yes, Sir."

He nodded and pulled the blindfold out of his bag. "I'm going to put this on. Do you need a pillow or anything for your neck?"

"No, Sir. I'm good, er, green." Her voice was soft.

Logan took the blindfold and put it over her eyes. "Lower your chin to your chest." When she did, he tied the blindfold behind her head. Then he made a few slight adjustments. "You can put your head back now."

"Oh my." Her words were so soft he almost didn't hear them. "I…" She jerked her arms, but they weren't going anywhere.

"Ellie." Logan leaned over and spoke in her ear. "Relax, sweetheart. I'm right here." Her shoulders slumped, and her breathing calmed. "That's it." He ran his fingers over her collarbone from where he stood behind her. "Feel my touch." The last thing he wanted her to do was panic.

He kept caressing her skin until he felt the tension leave her body, and she turned a nice rosy color. Her breathing, while still rapid, wasn't from panic but from excitement. Exactly what he wanted. He trailed his fingers to dip between her breasts.

Her gasp made him smile. Logan slipped his index finger beneath the fabric and traced the curve of her breast, one side and then the other before he delved in farther. Ellie shifted when he brushed her nipple.

"You're squirming," he said softly.

"Yes, Sir."

"Why?"

Her lips pursed together.

"Are you aroused?" He suspected Ellie was having trouble finding the right words. She was always so careful when speaking. He wanted her to talk dirty.

"Yes, Sir."

"Good. I want you to use your voice, Ellie. Tell me what you're feeling."

"Okay, Sir."

He toyed with her nipple until it was a hard bud before moving on to the other one. When both were hard nubs against her bra, he pinched them over the fabric. A soft cry left her lips, and she shifted.

"That feels so good, Sir."

"What does it feel like?"

"A pinch, then heat flowing through my breasts to the rest of my body, Sir."

Logan grinned at her words, pleased she was talking. Removing his hands from her breasts, he went to his bag and pulled out a vibrator. A special one. He'd bought this from Damon on a whim a while back. About three inches long and a half inch round, the tiny toy packed a punch, and it had a remote. Logan placed the remote on the table where he could reach it and cradled the toy in his palm to warm it up.

He knelt down next to the chair on her left side and stroked Ellie's stomach. She jumped. "You're so beautiful," he said softly. "Your skin is rosy, your nipples hard, and I can't wait to see how wet your pussy is."

Her stomach muscles tightened and released as he slid his fingers underneath her boy shorts, slowly inching toward her pussy. Using his middle finger, he stroked her outer pussy lips, giving her time to get used to his touch.

"How does this feel, sweetheart?"

"Good, Sir," she whispered.

Parting her pussy lips with his finger, he skimmed briefly over her clit, and then slid a finger into her wetness. A soft cry left her lips. "Oh goodness," she whispered.

"You feel so good. Soft, wet, and welcoming." He stroked with one finger for a few more moments before he added a second.

Ellie's hips shifted, but she wasn't going anywhere. He gave her a few more strokes, then slipped his fingers free, but kept them inside her shorts. Pushing against the fabric, he took the toy in his other hand and skimmed over her stomach to meet his other hand.

"Ummm, Sir, what is that?"

"One of my toys." He ran the toy around her pussy lips, coating it with her dew, before aligning the tip and pushing it into her.

Her mouth fell open on a gasp as he inserted the vibrating toy into her pussy, making sure it was well placed before he removed his hands.

He slipped his fingers into his mouth and tasted her sweet essence. His eyes closed in bliss, then he picked up the remote. "I did mention I would use toys."

"Yes, Sir." Her breathing had increased.

"How are your arms?"

She opened and closed her fingers. "Green, Sir."

"Good. We're going to start off at level one." Logan pressed the button.

Ellie's head jerked as the toy came to life. God, she was beautiful. Logan stood in front of her. "Focus on the sensations, Ellie." She couldn't see the crowd that had gathered to watch the scene.

He leaned down and brushed his lips against hers, before deepening the kiss, his tongue dueling with hers. He wanted to devour her, but that would be for another night. Logan broke the kiss, but stayed close.

"I can't wait to taste your pussy," he whispered, his breath brushing against her cheek. "You tasted so good on my fingers, I want to feast on you. I bet you taste exquisite when you come." He turned the toy up to the second level.

"Logan… Sir" she cried out.

"This toy has five levels; right now, we're on number two: strong but not super strong." He trailed his lips over her neck to kiss the top of her breasts before he took her hard, fabric-covered nipple in his mouth. He'd rather have her skin, but she wasn't ready for that yet.

He bit down gently, and she let out another cry. She was so responsive, even with the fabric between them.

"I can't…"

Logan lifted his head from where he left a wet spot on her bra to see her head shifting from side to side.

"What is it?"

"I…" Her body stiffened, and she cried out.

She climaxed from the toy. He hadn't expected that so quickly and instantly turned it off.

Ellie's mouth was open, and she was gasping for air.

"Ellie?"

She just shook her head. Logan didn't hesitate. He dropped the remote on the table, slipped his hand under her shorts and retrieved the toy. He removed the pin holding the chair legs out, brought her legs back together, and began untying them. He didn't think she was in distress, but something was off.

Once he was done there, he tossed the rope in his bag along with the remote and toy, then went to work on her arms. Ellie seemed to collapse into herself, her shoulders slumping, her arms lax in her lap. He grabbed a blanket and slipped it around her before he lifted her into his arms.

"It's okay, Ellie. I've got you." Her head lulled against his shoulder, and he realized he hadn't removed the blindfold. Once he had her in his lap, he untied the blindfold and took it off.

"Ellie? Sweetheart?" Her breathing had settled a bit, still choppy but slower. He checked her pulse, rapid but nothing to be alarmed about. Someone handed him a bottle of water. He took it without looking up, his focus on Ellie.

Her lashes rose, and she stared at him. "Damn, that was intense, Sir."

In that moment, Logan knew everything would be okay. He laughed. Ellie did that to him.

* * * *

Ellie snuggled against Logan's warm body. This man knew how to play her body like a well-tuned instrument. She'd never come so hard or fast from a toy before. But it was more than that. Being blindfolded heightened her other senses.

104

She heard everything. The murmurs of the crowd, the occasional slap of flesh hitting flesh, probably someone getting spanked. Then there was Logan's voice, whisky-smooth so that it flowed over her skin in a soft caress. His touch had been sure and gentle.

Even when he pinched her nipples, it wasn't a lasting pain. Just a slight twinge then pure pleasure. Ellie never thought she'd enjoy something like that. And that toy… Even though she couldn't see it, it felt like a bullet, but so much more powerful than any she'd ever used.

She shivered, and Logan tightened his arms around her, pulling the blanket closer. Ellie tilted her head back and gazed up into this handsome man's face. Every time she saw him, she was struck by his looks.

Yes, all the Doms in the club were lookers, but there was something about Logan's rugged features that drew her in.

"How are you doing?" His voice was husky.

"I'm good, Sir." Her body was settling down, and she'd begun to feel more like herself.

"Tell me what happened."

Ellie closed her eyes and rested her head against his shoulder. "I think you know, Sir." Her face grew hot.

"There's nothing to be embarrassed about. Remember: Pleasure is what we're both after. The club is about freedom. Freedom to relax and enjoy yourself without restraint."

"I think that happened, Sir." Logan chuckled, and Ellie couldn't suppress a smile. He was right. "I didn't expect to climax, Sir."

"Why not?"

She opened her eyes to see Logan staring down at her. "I…um…it usually takes more to make me orgasm, Sir."

His eyebrows rose. "Interesting." He stroked her arms. "Why do you think you were able to do so tonight?"

Ellie was going to answer that she didn't know, but stopped herself. Thinking back to their scene, she remembered each sensation, everything she was feeling when the answer hit her. "That's not possible," she whispered.

"What isn't, sweetheart?"

"Sorry, Sir. I was talking to myself." How could she explain? This was new to her as well. She'd only known Logan, what, about three weeks, unless she counted the time after Sierra's bachelorette party. But still, this was crazy to her.

"I can hear your brain working. Is it that hard to talk about?"

"A little bit, Sir." She'd never really had anyone to talk things out with, not since her brother died. Her heart clenched. What would her brother think of Logan? Her smile was wistful, even a little bittersweet. He'd like Logan. "I'm not sure of the protocol when it comes to talking about the men in my past." She didn't want Logan to think he didn't measure up or it was a competition.

"My ego can handle it." His voice was steady and sure.

"I haven't had many lovers, Sir. But I can tell you none have ever made me feel like you did tonight."

"And how did I make you feel?"

Lord, he wanted to know everything. But of course, communication was an important part of the lifestyle, as it should be in any relationship. "Safe, sexy, and worthy of your attention, Sir." There she said it.

"What the…" Logan's fingers closed over her chin. "Look at me, please."

Ellie opened her eyes to see his dark brown gaze filled with concern.

"You are sexy. You are safe with me. And you're more than worthy of my attention. No man should ever make you feel like you're not any of those three or anything less than the beautiful, caring woman you are." He shook his head. "Ellie, you are a woman to be cherished, loved, and…" He lowered his head, his words for her ears only. "Fucked any and every way she wants."

Heat flowed, and her pussy clenched. "Yes, Sir." The words slipped from her lips without conscious thought.

"Yes, what, sweetheart?"

"Fuck me, Sir." Ellie froze the second the words left her lips. She never talked like that.

Logan grinned. "I want to." His warm breath against her skin made her nerves come alive with anticipation of what he would do next. "It's too early, but we'll get there. I promise you."

"All right, Sir." She was trusting Logan with so much of her body right now, but it felt right, and she wasn't going to let fear hold her back. Logan was a police officer, and he could be killed in the line of duty, but that was a long shot.

Ellie knew the statistics. She'd researched them after her brother's death. She wanted to be with Logan, and something told her that her brother would approve. It was time for her to live her life without fear, and being with Logan would be the first step. With a sigh, she relaxed against him, enjoying his warmth and his arms around her. Tomorrow, she would worry about everything else.

* * * *

Logan sat on the sofa with Ellie in his arms, shock tinged with dismay about what she'd said. What the hell was wrong with the men in her life? He knew about her ex-husband, but others? Men put women down when they couldn't handle the self-confidence of a strong woman. He didn't understand that. Probably never would.

Maybe because he grew up secure in his ability to be himself and take care of others. He was never made to feel out of place like she was. Her family, except for her brother, didn't seem to have supported her. Well, he would change that.

He wanted to wrap Ellie up in his arms and never let her go. She'd shocked him when she said she wanted him to fuck her. Logan's lips twitched. Hearing the word *fuck* come from her lips made him want to grin from ear to ear. Not that what she said was funny. It's just that Ellie seemed all prim and proper and using words like that—even in a sexual situation—threw him.

Logan was excited to see where their relationship would go. Ellie was sexy and responsive to him, and he wanted to explore every part of her, to find out all her inner workings, and to make love to her over and over again. He wanted to show her how worthy she was and how sexy, too, and he would get that chance now. Any job was dangerous, and it wasn't like Pleasant Valley was a hotbed of crime. So yeah, maybe it was time to change his thinking about relationships and break his longstanding rule about not getting involved with a woman because of his job.

Chapter 8

Friday afternoon, Ellie stifled a yawn. It had been after one in the morning when Logan dropped her off at her apartment. She'd taken a quick shower, fallen into bed, and slept through her alarm. That had never happened before.

Maybe because she was so happy and satisfied last night, her brain finally turned off and allowed her to get some quality sleep. Luckily, today was an easy day. She'd been going through catalogs and calling around to arrange things for the Halloween party at the club.

Sierra had called her this morning to tell her it was a go. Ellie was a bit amazed she had persuaded Max to agree, but it did make her happy. This would be fun. The door to her shop opened, and she was surprised to see Tessa walking in.

"Hi, Tessa." Ellie stood up.

"Hi, Ellie, I hope you don't mind that I just dropped in."

"No. Please, come sit down." Ellie pulled out one of the chairs for Tessa, and then sat back down. "What can I do for you?"

"Sierra said she called you about the Halloween party."

"She did. I was just looking at stuff."

"I was wondering if I could help you with it?"

Ellie blinked. "This is unexpected."

"I know." Tessa twisted her hands together. "You know Sierra and Crystal are my best friends."

Ellie nodded. It was obvious when Crystal and Tessa convinced her to hold the bachelorette party in a strip club.

"Well. I've been wanting to do something special for the two of them."

"And you think the Halloween party is the right time?"

Tessa grinned, and Ellie froze. "I'm almost afraid to ask what you're planning."

Tessa laughed. "Nothing serious. What I was hoping was we could have some extra sexy props and a couple of dance poles. Plus music."

Ellie thought for a moment. "Props might not be too hard. For the dance poles, I'd have to measure and see if a portable one will work or if we need a ceiling mount. As for music, it would be easy enough to create a playlist but who can put it on the PA system?"

"I recruited Kaley for that. She'll take care of making sure the music is used."

"Okay." Ellie pulled her pad of paper over. "I was already planning on having fake spiderwebs everywhere. Along with cackling boxes for witches."

"Any way we can sex it up a bit? It is, after all, a party in a BDSM club."

Ellie chewed on the end of her pen. After last night, she had a better idea of what Tessa was getting at. "Let me check with a couple of vendors before I say more."

"Tell me." Tessa leaned closer.

"Well, I'm not sure, but I'm thinking of things the subs would enjoy and so would the Doms. Maybe using dildos or vibrators. It's an idea, but not sure exactly what I can get."

"Oh my god, that would be great. What else?"

"How about Dracula popping out of a coffin, but when he does, his cock is fully erect." Ellie was sure there was a way to make this work; she'd have to talk to her vendor, who was great with electronics. Boy, would he get a laugh out of this.

"Oh, that would be fun. Can you do some special lighting?"

"What are you thinking?"

"Usually, we just have subdued lighting, but I'd love to have some dance lights flashing around."

"Like disco lights?"

"Yeah, something that would flash around the room."

"Let me see what I can do. What else were you thinking?"

"Sierra mentioned male strippers."

"Yeah, but I'm not sure how we'd get them into the club, and with what goes on in the club, it might not be a good idea."

"What if we have some of the subs dress up with big strap ons."

"Oh my God, that's genius." Ellie jotted down some notes. "Do you know which subs yet? I can get the costumes for them."

"I can get names."

"Great. I know a wholesale guy who will sell us the costumes at cost, so we don't have to worry if they get ruined."

"Okay. We came up with a play list." Tessa opened her purse and pulled out a piece of paper. "Do you think you can put something together?"

Ellie scanned the list. "I can." Excitement flared in Ellie's stomach. This was going to be so much fun. She had her work cut out for her, but it would be fine. "Anything else?"

"I think that's it. Lara is doing the food, and Sierra is working with Max on invitations."

"How many people are we looking at?"

"Probably no more than seventy-five."

"I never asked, how many does the club hold?"

"Maximum capacity is about one-fifty, if I remember right. Oh, that reminds me. Do you think there is something we can do in the garden?"

"Garden?"

"Oh, you probably don't know about it yet. The club has a garden in back. When Max expanded the club, he had it put in."

"It depends on the weather, but I'll need to walk through it to see what we might be able to do."

Tessa rubbed her hands together. "I'll chat with Sierra. Maybe we can do it on a day when Max isn't around."

"That would work. Do you know how much Sierra has told Max?

Tessa's cheeks grew pink. "Yes. Not all the details, only that the ladies want to organize a Halloween party."

Ellie rolled her eyes. "You are all dangerous."

"You have no idea." Tessa's laughter floated through Ellie's shop.

"All right, let me get to planning this. The first of October is around the corner, and the next thing we know, it will be Halloween."

"Great." Tessa stood, and Ellie followed. "I'm so happy you're doing this." Tessa gave her a big hug. "Are you and Logan coming to the club tonight?"

"Yes." Logan told her they would be going. And somehow, she didn't mind that he told her instead of asking her. Another first in her life.

"Great. I'll be there with Damon."

Ellie walked Tessa to the door, waving as she climbed into her car and drove off. Well, she had a lot of work to do this afternoon.

* * * *

Ellie stored her stuff in the locker at Wicked Sanctuary that night as all the talk in the ladies' room floated over her. After her chat with Tessa, she made some phone calls. While she was in the club tonight, she'd pay special attention to how high the ceilings were.

She'd left messages with several of her vendors. They'd get back to her with the information she needed. Ellie also knew she needed to chat with Sierra about seeing the garden area and with Lara about food.

"You're glowing tonight," Tessa said.

"Planning mode." Ellie grinned.

"Ah, the Halloween party." Tessa kept her voice low.

"Yes."

"Which reminds me." Tessa clapped her hands, and the room fell silent. "Ladies, I need your attention for a moment. Ellie is going to plan a fun and sexy Halloween party. I need to know, by a show of hands, who would be willing to dress up in costume."

Hands shot up in the air. Ellie laughed. "Adventurous bunch."

"You have no idea," someone commented.

"I'll need names and sizes." Ellie reached into her locker and pulled out her cell to take notes. One by one, the women came up to her. By the time she was done, she had more volunteers than she needed.

Tossing her phone back in her purse, Ellie shut the locker, locked it, and followed Tessa out of the ladies' room.

"Thank you for doing this," Tessa said.

"Doing what?" Damon asked from where he lounged, leaning against the wall.

Tessa's face turned pink, surprising Ellie.

"Nothing, Sir. Just sub talk."

Ellie bit the inside of her lower lip. She could see the speculation in Damon's eyes.

"I see." Damon gestured for the women to walk ahead of him. "I'll get it out of you." The words were soft, but Ellie heard them. Then flesh hitting flesh.

Tessa jumped and yelped. Ellie glanced over her shoulder, and Damon grinned.

"That's what happens when subs don't behave. They get spanked."

Ellie nodded.

"Please don't scare her." Tessa turned to Damon. "We all know you're a pussy cat."

Damon stiffened, and Ellie held her breath.

"We'll see who's the pussy cat after our scene tonight."

"I can't wait," Tessa said as they moved into the club.

Ellie watched the couple walk away.

"You're frowning. What's wrong?" Logan asked, coming up to her.

"Just something Damon said." Ellie allowed Logan to lead her away from the doors and over to the bar area.

"Did he say something inappropriate to you?"

"No." She shook her head. "I'm pretty sure Tessa would lay him flat if he ever did. It's—" She broke off to gather her thoughts. "I'm still getting used to some of the sexual innuendos the Doms use."

"I see." Logan helped her onto one of the bar stools, then took the one next to her. "Are you worried? I can promise you Damon would never hurt Tessa."

"How can you promise that?"

"Because I know these men." Logan paused as Kaley stepped over to them from behind the bar.

"Can I get you two anything?" Kaley asked.

"Water for Ellie."

"You got it." Kaley reached down and set a water bottle in front of him. "Here you go, Sir."

Logan picked up the bottle, opened it, and set it in front of her. He was being a little high handed in ordering her water, but Ellie had observed Doms liked to do things for their subs. Logan was no different. And they were in the club.

"Thanks. I sometimes have trouble with the caps for some reason." She took a sip of the water. "What are we doing tonight?"

"Protocols."

"Sorry, Sir." Why did she keep forgetting that? He nodded, but his gaze stayed on her face. Ellie squirmed.

"Tonight, I think we're going to watch different scenes. I want you to see more of the club."

"I don't understand, Sir. We've watched scenes before."

"Yes. But tonight, we're going to watch, and not only are you going to tell me what you're seeing and feeling, I'm going to be touching you."

Excitement slid along her spine. "Yes, Sir."

"If you see something that bothers you or you're uncomfortable with, you are to voice it. Do not stay quiet."

"Yes, Sir."

"Don't answer so quickly, Ellie." He brushed a finger over her cheek. "I mean it. If I see you becoming uncomfortable and not speaking up, there will be consequences."

Her excitement was muted by apprehension. What were they going to watch tonight? Yes, she was new, and she had a lot of hard limits, but she wondered what he was talking about. "I'll tell you, Sir."

"Good. Grab your bottle of water, and let's go watch our first scene." He slid off the stool and held his hand out to her. Ellie released a breath, put her hand in his, and grabbed the water with her other hand. Tonight was going to be interesting.

Chapter 9

Logan escorted Ellie around the club. They'd viewed several scenes. Bondage and flogging and she was good with those. But when he stopped at one where a Dom had the sub on the wheel spinning her around, Ellie asked him if they could leave.

He took her into the quiet area. "What bothered you about that last scene?"

"It didn't seem like the sub had much control. Her Dom was spinning her around and around, Sir."

"Ah." He positioned them so they could see the scene from where they were sitting. "I want you to look at them, please." He waited until her gaze was on the couple. "That's Bennett and Harper. They play together almost exclusively."

"Are they a couple, Sir?"

"Not that I know of. They are play partners. I want you to watch Harper. Does she look scared?"

He held back a chuckle at the fierce concentration on Ellie's face. She did everything with her whole being.

"No, Sir."

"And Bennett?"

"His lips are moving, but I can't hear what he's saying. He's also touching her even as he spins her around, Sir."

"Correct. Harper likes it when Bennett takes control out of her hands. The spider web, as we call it, does that for her."

"I think I understand, Sir."

"It's okay if their kink is not your kink. We're all different people and like different things."

Ellie nodded. "I get it, Sir. I didn't mean to be judgmental."

"You didn't understand the dynamic, and it's going to happen. The important thing was that you asked to leave. I could tell it bothered you and wanted to know why."

"So much communication, Sir."

"Yes." He ran his fingers over her cheek. "Now let's go check out another scene."

He claimed a stool in front of another scene about to be played out. He helped Ellie onto the stool and stood behind her, her back against his front. He hoped her reaction to this scene was positive.

Damon and Tessa walked onto the stage. Damon set his bag down, and they talked quietly off to one side before Tessa shimmied out of her leather skirt, leaving her in a thong and a black strapless leather bra. Damon grabbed some rope and other restraints out of his bag before he led her over to the bondage system.

Logan leaned forward and whispered, "Did you notice them talking before the scene?"

"Yes, Sir."

"I will always talk with you about what we'll be doing, either before our night starts or once we're in the club."

"Doesn't that eliminate the element of surprise, Sir?"

"The more we're together, the less talking we'll need. Damon and Tessa have been together for months. They know each other, so their little talk, I'm sure, was a reminder about safe words."

"Do all Doms do that, Sir?"

"Do what, sweetheart?"

"Remind the sub of their safe words, Sir."

"In Wicked Sanctuary, yes. Most use the common green, yellow, and red, but a few of the subs have special safe words. It helps everyone stay safe."

"Okay, Sir."

Logan returned his attention to scene. Damon was restraining Tessa's arms in the bondage system. He finished, leaned over, and slipped his hands behind Tessa's back. Tessa's bra went flying across the stage to land where Damon's bag sat.

Ellie gasped.

"Easy. Remember, this is all consensual."

"Yes, Sir."

Logan rested his hands on Ellie's shoulders. She was tense, her breathing increased. "You haven't seen this bondage system in play before. It's modular; right now, Damon is using it like the bondage chair, but I suspect later he'll use the other parts and give Tessa a nice flogging."

Now Damon was restraining Tessa's legs, but only at her ankles. Logan wondered what Damon had in store for his sub. After making sure Tessa was all right, Damon went over to his bag and pulled several things out.

Ellie stiffened at the sight of Damon's toys. Logan chuckled softly.

"He won't hurt her."

"But, Sir…"

Logan slid his hands down to her collarbone. "Damon knows what he's doing, and look at Tessa. Does she look worried?"

"No, Sir. She appears to be relaxed."

"Yes. She trusts her Dom."

Ellie nodded.

"I'll explain what Damon is doing." Damon set everything on the small table and said something to Tessa, who giggled.

"Damon has picked up a set of nipple clamps. Did you see how Tessa wiggled in her seat?"

"Yes, Sir."

"Anticipation of what her Dom is about to do to her."

"Those look painful, Sir."

"Does Tessa look afraid?"

"No, Sir. She actually looks excited."

"Good girl. Yes, she knows exactly what to expect from those clamps." He watched as Damon slipped the clamps on Tessa's hard nipples and tightened them until she let out a gasp.

"He's hurting her, Sir." Ellie shifted on the stool.

"Does she look like she's in pain?" Logan wanted Ellie to understand the difference between pain and pleasure.

Ellie tilted her head. "No, Sir," she answered after a moment.

"I'm not going to say Tessa didn't feel some pain when Damon first tightened them, but he knows how much pressure to apply to keep her feeling pleasure." Logan returned his gaze to the scene.

Ellie dropped her chin to her chest as Damon opened the legs of the chair and revealed Tessa was wearing a crotchless thong.

"Ellie?"

"He's putting her on display, Sir." Her voice was soft.

"And why is that bothering you?" She'd seen a lot of people undressed in the club.

"She's my friend, Sir."

So that was it. "Ellie, Tessa has lots of friends in the club. Look around, you'll see Sierra and Max watching the scene, along with a lot of other people Tessa knows in the club."

Ellie turned her head from one side to the other, then she turned to look at him. "I don't understand, Sir."

"Wicked Sanctuary is a safe place to be who you are. No one here will judge you for anything. We're all adults."

"I think I get it, Sir."

He gave her an out if she needed it. "Do you want to keep watching or stop?"

"No, Sir. I want to stay."

Logan brushed a soft kiss over her cheek. "That's my girl."

Ellie's cheeks turned pink. He moved back behind her and looked at the stage.

Damon had a vibrator in his hand. Tessa shook her head. "No, Sir. Please."

"Oh princess, I did warn you." Damon held the vibrator up. "This is a toy of my own invention. You'll notice it's not overly big, but it will get the job done, because not only does it vibrate, it also revolves." He switched it on. The women groaned, and the men chuckled. "My lady here goes crazy with this one." Damon leaned over and placed the toy at her entrance and pushed it all the way in. Then he closed her legs around it and stepped back.

"Fuck," Tessa cried out as Damon pressed the remote in his hand.

"It's on low at the moment. I'm going to let her warm up a bit before I turn it higher."

"Sir?" Ellie said softly.

"Yes." Her skin was flushed, and her breathing had increased. Good. She was getting excited by what she was seeing. Not all women were visual, but it seemed Ellie was.

"I don't understand. Why did he close her legs around the toy, Sir?"

"To keep the toy in place." Logan stepped in front of Ellie, then knelt down. He put his hands on the inside of her knees. Ellie nodded, and he pushed them apart. "You see, sometimes, especially with certain toys, when your pussy muscles clamp down, they can push the toy out." He lightly traced the seam of her shorts over her slit.

"Oh." Her breath whooshed out of her, but she didn't try to close her legs.

"Pleasure is the goal." He removed his hand and stood up.

* * * *

The second Logan removed his hand and stood, Ellie missed him. She'd never considered herself a visual person as far as being aroused, but it was happening tonight. Her nipples were hard against her bra, and her pussy tingled.

She was having trouble watching because it was Tessa, but Logan was right. No one here would judge, and she wasn't passing judgment either. She watched as Damon circled Tessa, occasionally flicking the nipple clamps or caressing her skin.

All activity was done in a loving manner, and that was what she focused on. Damon's touch looked soft and made to arouse—not hurt. Tessa's eyes would drift shut then open, and she would wiggle in the bondage chair. Not that she could go anywhere.

"I think it's time to get these off," Damon said. He leaned over and took one of the nipple clamps off, then covered Tessa's nipple and the area around it with his mouth. Tessa let out a small cry, but that was it. Then he did the same with her other nipple. This time, Tessa didn't make a sound, but Ellie could hear her rapid breathing.

"Sir, why did he cover her nipple with his mouth?"

"When he took the clamp off, blood rushed back to her nipple, and the nipple would be very sensitive. Damon is helping her feel more pleasure than pain."

Ellie watched Tessa carefully. Her eyes were closed, her mouth open as if she couldn't get enough air, but she didn't seem to be in pain. There were so many aspects of the lifestyle Ellie hadn't thought of.

Damon dropped the clamps in his bag then pressed on the remote in his hand. "Sir!" Tessa cried out.

"Since your eyes are closed, you can't see what I did. I turned up the vibrations, but also started the vibrator turning. For those of you in the audience, these will be on sale in a few months. I'm still making some modifications. Tessa is my test subject."

There was some chuckling. "That's the second time he's mentioned making toys. Does Damon make all his toys, Sir?"

"He does. He also owns the adult shop, Kleinman's."

Ellie nodded. She'd been to the adult store but had forgotten Damon owned it. Not that it bothered her. "How does he sell his toys, Sir?" She couldn't quite picture Damon selling them in his own store, but he probably could.

"Internet. He has built up quite a following. He started making his toys when he was at MIT."

"That's a long time, Sir." Damon looked to be in his thirties, and he'd been doing this while in college?

"He's perfected his toys but is always coming up with new ones." Logan's breath brushed her ear. "Tell me what Tessa looks like to you."

Ellie took a deep breath and let it out. "Her eyes are closed, Sir. Her head is resting against the wood behind her head, and she's squirming in her seat."

"What else?"

Tilting her head, Ellie studied Tessa. "Her skin is flushed, Sir. Oh and her legs are slightly parted. She's also breathing hard."

"And Damon?"

"He's watching her, Sir. Keeping his gaze on her at all times and occasionally stroking her skin."

"He's letting her know he's there, making sure she's safe and cared for."

Another interesting tidbit, the touching. It was then Ellie realized that Logan was lightly caressing her upper arms. She'd been concentrating on the couple so much she hadn't really felt his touch. Or had she? He was becoming familiar. It wasn't a bad thing; she liked the idea of his touch.

"Please, Sir. No more," Tessa said, moving her head from side to side.

"Oh, we're not done yet." Damon tapped the remote, and Tessa let out a cry.

"I'm…" Tessa began shaking. She was trying to move her hips and open and close her legs. Her toes were pressed hard against the floor.

"She's going to topple backward," Ellie said softly.

"It's bolted down. One of the safety features Max put in when a male sub almost pushed the unit over. The legs move as do other parts, but the base is bolted."

"Thank goodness, Sir."

Logan rubbed his cheek against hers. "Would you enjoy it if I played with you in that chair? Made you climax for the audience?"

Ellie swallowed. Her pussy tingled with his words. She was aroused. It didn't shock her, but it did surprise her. Was it the scene or Logan?

Fingers closed over her fabric-covered breasts. "Beautiful breasts. Firm, with nipples that remind me of small raspberries."

The next thing she knew, his fingers were beneath the fabric, toying with her nipples. They stiffened beneath his touch.

"Sir," she said softly.

"Do you like what I'm doing?"

"Yes, Sir." She did. Logan's skin was slightly rough against hers. She shivered in pleasure and anticipation.

"I'm glad, because I want to do a lot more."

"Like what, Sir?" She was surprised she asked the question. But now that she had, she wanted to know his answer.

"That's a very loaded question. Are you sure about this?"

"Very much so, Sir."

"All right." Logan shifted behind her, he slipped his hand from her bra and moved over her stomach, to the top of her shorts. He slipped one hand under the fabric. "We've barely scratched the surface so far. Once we're alone, I want to strip you out of these clothes."

Her breath caught as his fingers slipped down to the top of her mound.

"Once you are naked, I'd place you on the bed and have you spread your legs, where I can see your pussy."

He slid one finger over her wet folds. Ellie squirmed in her seat.

"Be still."

"Yes, Sir." She shifted so her feet were solidly against the floor.

"Now I'm crawling up between your legs. I can smell your wetness. I part those pussy lips, and I dip my head."

His tongue swept over her ear. Ellie jumped as sensations shot throughout her body. His words were turning her on.

"I lick up your sweet cream, and I tongue fuck you until you're moaning."

She had to bite her lip to stop a groan from leaving her lips.

"I love how wet you are." He pushed a finger into her wet core. "I'm hoping it's because you want me."

"I do, Sir." Ellie could barely catch her breath. Her reaction to Logan was outside her normal experience.

"Good. Once I've thoroughly tongue fucked you, I'm going to slip my fingers into you." Another finger joined the first. "Spread your legs."

Ellie didn't even think about it; her legs parted.

"Feel my fingers in you. Stroking you." His words matched his movement.

"Oh goodness." She could barely breathe. Ellie opened her mouth, hoping to get more air into her lungs.

"I'm going to fuck you with my fingers and make you come." Her pussy muscles tightened around his finger. "So wet and so ready."

Even though she still had her shorts on, he was able to move his fingers in and out of her pussy, then his thumb was on her clit.

"Logan… Sir"

"Right here. How does that feel?"

"Decadent, Sir."

"Just decadent?" He curved his fingers inside her pussy.

"Oh, God, Sir." Ellie couldn't help herself. She shifted her hips forward, pushing down on his fingers.

"Come for me, Ellie."

He rubbed circles on her clit with his thumb as his fingers in her pussy pressed hard against her g-spot. Ellie clamped her teeth together as her world fell apart. The sounds of her pleasure were muted as Logan took her over the top and then guided her down the other side.

Her head fell forward as she panted. He'd made her climax. In the club. Again. She jerked her head up. No one was looking at them; the audience was watching the couple on the stage as Tessa screamed out her orgasm.

"Next time, you'll be more vocal," Logan whispered as he slid his fingers from her shorts, leaving a trail of wetness.

"Vocal?" Her throat was dry.

"Yes. Look at me."

Ellie didn't try to resist. She leaned her head back until she was gazing at Logan's face. His eyes blazed with passion. He lifted his hand and placed his fingers between his lips, then dragged them over his lower lip.

"Pure ambrosia," he whispered before leaning down and brushing a kiss over her lips. "I can't wait to have you at my mercy."

"I don't think I can either, Sir."

His eyes flared with desire. "Don't say things like that when I can't do anything about them."

"I don't understand, Sir."

"You're not ready for what I want to do to you in the club."

"Then let's go someplace private, Sir."

"Are you sure you're ready for that?"

Ellie lifted her hand, put it on the back of Logan's neck, and tugged. When he was close enough, she kissed him. She didn't censor herself but let him know through that kiss she was ready to have him in her bed.

He looked somewhat stunned when she broke the kiss. She took a deep breath when she saw the heat in his eyes.

"Let's get the heck out of here." He tugged her off the stool and out of the club. "Five minutes. Get your stuff and meet me here."

"Yes, Sir." Logan swatted her on the butt as she walked into the ladies' room. Thank goodness she could pull her street clothes on over her club wear.

Chapter 10

In record time, she walked out of the ladies' room. Logan was waiting for her, and he took her bag and captured her hand with his. They said good night to Ralph and made their way to Logan's SUV. He helped her in before throwing their bags in back.

Once he was behind the wheel, he looked at her. "You don't have to work tomorrow?"

"I'm good. Everything is covered."

He nodded, took her hand again, and began driving.

Ellie loved holding hands with Logan. It kept her grounded and didn't allow her to worry too much about what she was doing. She usually wasn't so bold, but the past few weeks had taught her she could be who she was around Logan, and he wouldn't judge her for it.

I'm free. The words echoed in Ellie's brain. She was free. Free to do what she wanted and be herself. A weight she hadn't known she'd been carrying was lifted, and her body relaxed.

When he turned left as they hit town, she glanced out the window, noticing the flashes of the street lights on the pavement. She turned to Logan.

"Where are we going?"

"My place."

Anticipation burned in her belly. "Okay." She couldn't wait to see where he lived.

He pulled into the driveway of a small ranch-style home. The outdoor lights gleamed against the pale brown paint. The garage door opened, and he pulled in, shut off the engine, and pressed the button on the fob to close the garage door.

She watched him get out of the car and walk around the front of his vehicle. Her heart picked up speed. His home. If he was anything like her, and she suspected he was, his home was his private retreat. She was happy he decided to share it with her. Logan opened her door and helped her out before grabbing their bags. Keeping her hand in his, he led her to the door.

He opened the door and flipped on the light. "Welcome to my home."

Ellie followed him through the utility room to the door into the main house. Logan opened the second door and gestured for her to proceed. Ellie took a deep breath and slipped past him into a small hallway.

Logan flipped on more lights. "Kitchen and family room to the left, bedrooms to the right. I'll give you the grand tour later." He nudged her to the right, and Ellie took the hint.

The bedroom to her right was dark, and Logan guided her to the room at the end of the hallway.

"Master bedroom," he said.

Soft light filled the room from the lamp beside the bed. "This room is huge." Her gaze darted around the room. A king-sized bed filled one area of the room, a TV mounted on the wall across from it.

A large dresser graced another wall, along with a recliner in front of the window. On the other wall was a long bench. Logan deposited their bags on the bench and slipped off his shoes. Ellie watched as he moved over to the bed and threw the green and brown comforter back to reveal tan sheets.

She swallowed as she slipped off her shoes, making sure to set them next to Logan's. She turned, and he was staring at her with such heat her body instantly caught fire.

"I'm on birth control, and the recent tests I was required to take for admission to the club were negative. I hadn't been with anyone for quite a while prior to the tests and no one after the tests."

"I was tested less than a month ago with negative results. I haven't been with anyone since the tests were done. I want to take this slow, but you're very aroused."

"How do you know that?" This man had already brought her to climax once tonight; how could she be so ready for him again. Okay, it had been about a thirty-minute drive to his house from the club, but she'd never reacted like this.

Logan smiled. "You're breathing is rapid; your skin flushed. Your pupils are dilated, and I can see you fidgeting. Arousal suits you."

Fire swept through her face.

"Ellie." His hands closed over her shoulders. "Never be embarrassed about wanting me or about your own sensuality."

She reached up and cupped his cheek. "I've never been with a man as open as you are."

"I have a feeling there are going to be a lot of firsts tonight." He moved his hand to the hem of her shirt and lifted it up and off. "If you haven't guessed, I'm going to undress you now

"Please," she whispered.

Passion flared hotter in his eyes as his fingers moved to her pants. He swept them down her legs and pulled them off along with her socks. When he stood, his fingers trailed up the back of her legs, and his palms settled on her ass.

"Your skin is so soft," he whispered before his lips captured hers. Ellie instantly parted her lips to his. His tongue swept in, tasting, touching, dueling with hers. Her arms curved around his neck.

She wanted Logan more than she'd wanted any other man. He lit a spark inside her that wouldn't go out. Her hands slid from around his neck to his chest, stroking his well-defined pecs beneath the fabric of his shirt until she reached his belt and waistband. Ellie started pulling his shirt out of his pants.

He broke the kiss. "Bad girl," he whispered. "Did I say you could undress me?" He unsnapped her bra and swept it away.

"No." She gazed up at him. Should she add the *Sir*? They weren't in the club.

"Then behave yourself." He released her. "On the bed, sweetheart."

Ellie looked at the bed and back to Logan. "I don't think I can." The bed was on a platform, and she wasn't quite tall enough to climb onto it. Logan was several inches taller than she was. He stared at her. "Logan, the bed is too high for me, and I don't see any steps."

Understanding dawned in his eyes. He clasped her around the waist and lifted her onto the mattress. "I'll get a step stool for you, but not right now."

"Why would you get me a step stool?"

"Because you're going to be spending time with me in this bed."

She should have been shocked at his declaration, but instead, it created a sense of anticipation and longing. "Where do you want me?"

"In the middle."

Ellie scooted to the middle of the bed and turned her head to watch Logan as he stripped out of his clothes. First, the shirt went over his head, showing off his sculpted chest. Not that she hadn't seen it before; he'd been bare chested at the club.

His fingers went to his pants. Ellie swallowed. She could already see his cock straining against the fabric. He slid them down, and his dick sprang free. She bit her lip as he stepped out of his pants. The man was sculpted from head to toe.

"Ellie, you keep staring at me like that, and this is going to be a hard, quick fuck." His voice was husky.

"Sorry, I can't help it." She couldn't.

"Then let me give you something else to think about." He moved to the end of the bed and climbed onto the mattress. "Spread those legs for me."

Ellie didn't even think about it as she complied. He advanced until he was between her legs.

"You are so fucking beautiful." Logan stroked her inner thighs. "I can't wait to taste you."

Before Ellie could get a word out, he laved her mound. Her fingers curled into the covers as the sensations flooded her body. Logan continued to lick until she was squirming on the mattress.

"Like that, do you?" he remarked after lifting his head. "Then let's have some fun." He lowered his head again, but this time, he pushed two fingers into her pussy, and his tongue went to work on her clit.

"Damn," Ellie whispered as tingles flowed through her body. This man should be registered as a dangerous weapon.

Each press of his fingers and flick of his tongue took her higher and higher. All too soon, she was nearing the edge.

He removed his mouth and fingers from her. "Not yet," he whispered.

"Please." She was primed and ready.

"I want to be in you when you come."

Logan worked his way up her body, his hard cock brushing against her pussy. Desire hit her full force. "Take me," she whispered.

He brushed her hair way from her face. "You are a treasure." His lips captured hers as he positioned his cock at her entrance and pushed forward.

Ellie could barely breathe. Logan was so hard and thick. She wrapped her arms around his shoulders as their mouths devoured each other. Inch by inch, he slid into her.

Her pussy relaxed, and soon, he was fully seated inside her. Her fingers dug into his back as he lifted his head.

"So wet, so warm, so snug."

"You are hard and big."

Logan grinned as he pulled back and then thrust back inside her. Ellie closed her eyes and tightened her arms around him. Her nerves already danced with need. It wouldn't take much to push her over.

* * * *

Logan gazed down at Ellie's face. Her eyes were closed, but her breathing was choppy and her skin a nice rosy color. He continued to move in and out of her pussy. He wasn't kidding when he said she was warm and snug. Her pussy gripped him tight, and he loved every second of it.

He wanted to stay inside her, but first, he wanted to make her come and release the tension he could see building in her body. He rained kisses over her face as he moved faster.

With each thrust, his body tightened with passion and need. Soon. First, he wanted to feel her release, then he'd take his. Her nails dug into his back, and he didn't care. He'd proudly wear her marks.

As her pussy tightened around his cock, he kept up his pace, thrusting harder and harder.

"I'm going to come," Ellie whispered.

"Come for me, sweetheart."

The second the words left his mouth, her pussy clamped down on his cock, and she cried out. Her body convulsed underneath him. Damn, this woman was a wonder. He held still until her climax softened, then he began moving once again.

"Logan." Her eyes were open, her gaze on him.

"Yes." He moved leisurely, letting the tension in both of them build back up.

"I don't think I can come again."

"I bet you can." He hadn't even touched her clit as he fucked her, and she'd come.

She shook her head.

"Are you challenging me to prove you wrong?" He picked up his pace.

"No." She shook her head. "I just don't think…"

"Don't think. Just feel. Feel me, what you do to me and what I do to you."

Ellie groaned, but that wasn't about to stop him. His balls tightened with each thrust. He probably wouldn't last much longer, but he wanted her to enjoy this as well.

Logan slid his hand over her belly, down to her clit. He rubbed her with his thumb.

"Fuck, Logan." She bucked against him, driving his cock into her harder.

"This is all for you." He kept playing with her clit as he thrust into her. It didn't take long. Another cry left her lips as she tightened around his cock.

One, two… On the third thrust, he erupted inside her, his cock pulsing as her body squirmed against him.

When he finished, he rested against her, their harsh breathing filling the room. Logan gazed down at her. Ellie's eyes were closed, her lips open, her breathing labored. He started to pull away.

"No." Her arms tightened around his. "Stay."

"I'm too heavy." He slipped his arm between her and the mattress and rolled them onto their side.

"Damn," she whispered.

"Are you okay?"

"I love how you feel in me, but that little change made my body go nuts. Again. I don't think I can take any more."

He grinned. "You feel good to me too." Logan brushed the hair away from her face. They laid there for a while until their breathing became normal.

Ellie shifted, and his cock reacted. "Let me get us both cleaned up," he said. He slid from her warmth, climbed off the bed, and walked into the bathroom.

He cleaned himself up, then nabbed a new washcloth, wet it, and picked up a towel. He walked to the bed where Ellie lay, eyes closed. "Ellie, can you bend your leg so I can clean you, please."

"Don't want to move," she whispered.

"Come on, baby." He nudged her leg with his free hand. Slowly, she bent her knee and lifted her leg. He made quick work of cleaning her up, took the towel and washcloth back in the bathroom, and made his way back to her.

He climbed onto the bed and pulled her into his arms. She snuggled close to him as he slipped the sheet over them.

He kissed her forehead, and she made a noise. Something between a sigh of pleasure and a groan. Logan closed his eyes, loving the feeling of Ellie's body against his. Her head on his chest. A contentment he hadn't ever felt before filled him. Maybe being in a relationship wasn't so bad.

Chapter 11

Ellie unlocked her shop on Monday with a smile. She'd spent the weekend with Logan and damn, that man had stamina. They'd spent most of Sunday cuddling on his sofa, watching football and talking. She was happy. Happier than she'd ever been.

Logan was good for her, and she wasn't going to worry over what he did for a living. Her brother's death was tragic. She knew that deep down, and she refused to borrow trouble.

She made some phone calls to get things lined up for the Halloween party at the club. Ellie needed to call Sierra and find a day when she could do a walk-through of the gardens so she could plan that out as well.

Later that afternoon, her cell rang. She glanced at the display. Sierra. "Perfect timing, I was just about to call you."

"Ellie, it's Max."

Ellie took a deep breath. "Hello, Max."

"Sierra is driving; that's why I'm on her phone."

"Okay. What's up?" Max sounded stressed, which wasn't like him.

"Just tell her," Ellie heard Sierra say.

"Ellie, I just got a call from Logan's sergeant."

The world stopped turning as her grip tightened on her phone.

"Logan was hurt on the job. Sierra and I are on our way to Pleasant Valley Hospital right now. We're almost to your shop. We'll pick you up."

Ellie closed her eyes and fought against the panic inside her. "No. I'll see you there."

"No, Ellie." Max's voice was hard. "You will wait for us. We're less than five minutes away. If you so much as try to drive, I'll make sure Logan spanks your ass so hard you won't sit down for a week."

Ellie swallowed. "Yes, Sir."

"Good girl."

She ended the call and grabbed her purse. Her heart was pounding so hard, she was sure it would burst. By the time Max and Sierra pulled into the parking lot, she'd locked up and was outside. Max helped Ellie into the passenger seat and switched places with Sierra.

Sierra patted Ellie's shoulder from the back seat. "It will be okay, Ellie."

Ellie forced herself to breathe as Max drove. Nausea and anxiety rolled through her during the ten minute drive to the hospital. Logan had to be okay. He had to be. She tangled her fingers together in her lap to stop the shaking.

"What exactly did his sergeant say?" If she could concentrate on talking, maybe she wouldn't want to scream.

"Not much. Only that Logan was hurt, and I was on his emergency call list." Max went around another car.

That wasn't much. Damn. How bad was it? If anything happened to Logan— She needed more information. Sierra was quiet in the backseat, and Max's stoic features didn't reveal anything. What could they say? They didn't know any more than she did. Dread filled her gut.

Ellie wanted assurances that Logan would be okay, but no one could say that with any certainty right now. The emergency room entrance came into view.

Max pulled up to the doors, and Ellie didn't wait. She jumped out of the car and ran for the doors. It was a miracle her shaking legs held her up. "Logan Wolfe," she gasped out at the counter. She could barely say his name as tears welled.

"And you are?" the nurse asked.

"His fiancée," Sierra said coming up beside her.

Ellie didn't correct the lie. She needed to see that Logan was all right. Oh, God. What if he was dead? Her knees almost buckled.

The nurse nodded. "Go in and to the right."

"Thank you." Sierra took her arm as the doors opened. They turned right and went down the hall to a waiting room filled with several officers.

"Oh God," Ellie whispered as she staggered. It was her brother's death all over again. No. She couldn't think that way. While the men were stoic, they didn't have the devastated look of having lost a friend.

"Easy." Sierra led her into the room.

All eyes turned to them, and Ellie froze. She wasn't sure she could do this.

"Ms. Tanner, I'm Sergeant Jenson." The older man held out his hand.

"Sergeant?" Ellie could barely talk. "How do you know who I am?"

"Logan has mentioned you. I didn't have your number." He glanced at Sierra.

"Sierra Preston. Max is my husband."

"Mrs. Preston." The sergeant shook her hand. "We're waiting for news."

"How bad?" Ellie asked.

"A minor accident. It's protocol for paramedics to be called and for him to be checked out."

For the first time in what felt like hours, Ellie could take a breath. "Thank you." Sierra started to lead her over to a chair.

"I can't sit." Ellie turned. "How minor of an accident? Did they say how long this was going to take?" Minor accidents to could turn into a major issue, even death.

Sergeant Jenson shook his head. "I haven't received a full report. They're doing all the normal testing. That's all I know at the moment."

Ellie wanted to scream. She knew it wouldn't help, so she bit back her words and her frustration. Max walked in, nodded to the sergeant, and made a beeline for her and Sierra.

"Ellie, why don't you sit down," Max said softly.

"I can't." Her stomach cramped. "What if Logan is seriously hurt or dying?" This time, she couldn't stop the overflowing tears.

"He's not," Max said, his voice firm.

"You can't know that." Her voice rose. What was she going to do without Logan? This was worse than when her brother died.

"Ellie." Max put his hands on her shoulders. "I checked with one of the nurses. He's alive."

"For how long?" While that was good news, it didn't mean he was out of the woods. Ellie was well aware she was in full on panic mode, but couldn't seem to pull out of it.

"Don't borrow trouble," Max said. "Logan is healthy and strong."

"Max is right," Sierra piped up.

Ellie glanced around the room. The officers there were sober. Too sober. She wasn't sure how much hope she had left in her. "I…" She broke off as the door opened and a doctor walked in.

"Is there an Ellie Tanner here."

"That's me." She slid past Max.

"Mr. Wolfe is asking for you."

"Is he…" She couldn't get any words past her lips.

"He's got a concussion and bruised his tailbone, but he'll make a full recovery." A big sigh was heard through the room. "He's asking for you," he told Ellie.

"Let's go." She took a step forward.

"Ellie." Max put his hand on her shoulder. "Are you going to be okay alone?"

She straightened her shoulders. "I'll be fine." At least she hoped so. The doctor opened the door and gestured for her to precede him. Max released her, and she walked through the door.

"Room fourteen." The doctor pointed the way and followed behind her.

The curtain was pulled, and Ellie hesitated. The doctor reached around her and held the curtain back. Ellie lifted her head and walked in.

Logan lay in the hospital bed, his eyes closed, his face pale. There was an IV in his right arm and monitors hooked up for his vitals. Ellie barely kept upright and had to fight to keep herself from faceplanting as she approached the bed.

"Logan, I'm here," she said softly.

His eyes opened. "Hi, my lady."

Him saying *my* lady caused the tears she'd been fighting to fall.

"Oh, baby." He reached for her.

"No, don't hurt yourself." She stepped back. The last thing she wanted to do was hurt him more.

"I'm fine. Come here." He held his hand out to her.

She took his hand, and he tugged her closer. "Head on my chest, so you can see for yourself my heart is strong."

Ellie hesitated, but the command in Logan's voice weakened her knees further. She laid her head on his chest and gently hugged him. The monitor started beeping faster, and Ellie started to back away, but Logan curved his left arm around her. "Best medicine ever."

"I shouldn't be lying on you."

"I need you here. I don't give a damn about anyone else." His voice was rough.

"Logan." His heartbeat was strong beneath her ear, and her tears continued to fall, soaking his gown.

"I'm okay. Please stop crying. It's killing me."

"What?" She forced her head up.

"I can't stand to see you cry like this."

Ellie sniffled. "Sorry if my fear isn't to your liking." How dare he? Didn't he understand how much this upset her?

"That isn't what I meant." Logan slid his hand up to the back of her neck. "I don't think you heard me. I'm perfectly all right."

"They have you hooked up to an IV and machines. The doctor said you had a concussion and a bruised tailbone. I would say that isn't all right."

"Sweetheart, the IV and heart monitor are protocol. Outside of a headache, I'm fine. I swear it."

Ellie so wanted to believe him "Tell me what happened."

"A silly mistake my partner made."

"What does that mean?" She needed answers.

"I can't discuss it until I talk with my boss. Let's just say he did something he shouldn't have, and it resulted in me getting knocked on my ass."

"They don't bring you to the hospital for simply getting knocked down."

Someone cleared their throat, and they both looked toward the door where the doctor stood. "Mr. Wolfe, I need your permission before I explain to Ms. Tanner what's happened."

"You have it."

Ellie straightened and pulled the chair over close to the bed and sat down, her hand still in Logan's.

"Ms. Tanner, Mr. Wolfe's injuries are minor."

"What kind of injuries?" Logan squeezed her fingers.

"Minor. He went down hard on concrete and was momentarily disoriented. Initial assessment was he'd hit his head and was only momentarily unconscious. He was transported here for further tests."

"And?" she asked.

"I have everything back now. He's cleared for discharge. Nothing broken. Minor concussion. No skull fracture and no sign of swelling in the brain. He'll have a headache for a day or two, and his tail bone will be sore. I'm sure he'll have some bruising still to appear. There's no reason to keep him in the hospital."

For the first time since Max called her, Ellie could take a full breath. "Thank God," she whispered.

"I'll write up your discharge instructions. I want you to go home and rest, but you'll need someone to stay with you for at least twenty-four hours. There may be some mild dizziness, but any nausea and/or vomiting, I want you back here."

"Trust me, he will be." Ellie wasn't going to let Logan out of her sight.

The doctor nodded and left the room.

"See? Everything is fine." Logan squeezed her fingers again.

"This time. What about next time?" Her heart pounded. Would things turn out this good the next time something like this happened?

"Honey." Logan's voice was gentle. "I can't promise there won't be another incident, but it's been a very long time since the Pleasant Valley PD had an officer die on duty."

"Maybe, but…" Ellie shook her head.

"Ellie." His voice grew deeper. "Look at me."

She turned her head, and their gazes met.

"I don't take chances. I'm very careful in my job."

"But you can't predict what others will do."

"No, I can't. I can only promise you I'm as careful as I can be. I'm not saying accidents don't happen, but I do everything in my power to make sure they don't."

Ellie nodded, but her heart was heavy. She needed a few minutes to herself. "I should go let the others know you're okay."

"I'm sure the doctor told them."

"I want to be sure." Ellie detangled her hand from his. While part of her didn't want to leave, she had to for her own mental health. "I'll be back in a few minutes."

Logan nodded. Ellie left the room and went back to the waiting room. When she walked in, Sierra embraced her. "Logan okay?"

"Yes." Ellie swallowed her tears. She glanced around the room to Logan's boss. "Minor concussion and bruised tailbone. They're discharging him."

"Good. I'll check in with him later and get all the information I need from him. Tell him to go home and rest." The sergeant looked at the other man, who nodded, and they both left the room.

"Max." Ellie turned her attention to him. "Would you drive Logan and me to Logan's place. I'll find a way to get my car from my shop later."

"Of course, I'll drive you both. As for your car, give me the keys, and I'll make sure it gets to Logan's place so you have transportation."

"Thank you." Ellie dug her spare key out of her purse. Thank goodness she kept it in her purse just in case she left her keys in her car.

"How long before he's discharged?" Sierra asked.

"Not sure. The doctor was getting things going, and the nurses have to unhook the IV and stuff." Ellie shrugged. What more could she say? Her brain was still racing with the what-if scenarios.

"I'll go check," Max said and left the room.

"Come sit down." Sierra put her arm around Ellie's shoulders and guided her to a large bench. Sierra kept her arm around her shoulders after they sat down. Ellie was grateful for her support because she felt like she was one second away from a meltdown.

* * * *

Logan looked up when Max entered the room. The nurses had already removed the IV and the heart monitor. He'd already put his pants on, not that it would have mattered. Max had seen it all.

"Where's Ellie?"

"In the waiting room with Sierra. I was just coming to see how long things would take."

Logan was disappointed not to see Ellie, but he understood she might need some time. He'd been aware of her panic. "I'm just waiting for the discharge information, and then we can spring me from this place." He wasn't overly fond of hospitals, plus he wanted to get back to Ellie to show her he really was all right.

"Great."

A nurse walked in pushing a wheel chair. "Mr. Wolfe, here are your discharge papers. As the doctor told you, any nausea, vomiting, or increased dizziness, return to the ER. If you need something for pain, you can use ibuprofen or acetaminophen."

"Thank you." Logan took the papers from her and looked at the wheelchair.

"Protocol," the nurse said.

Logan sighed, settled himself, and placed his feet on the metal holders.

"I'll tell the ladies and go get the car."

By the time the nurse had wheeled him to the doors of the hospital, Sierra and Ellie had joined them.

"Should I take a picture of Logan?" Sierra whispered. "The guys at the club would have a nice laugh."

"Don't you dare," Logan said, glancing up at the women.

"Don't worry. I'll protect your manliness," Ellie said, amusement in her voice. Her eyes widened, as if she'd surprised herself as well.

Logan took her hand and raised it to her lips, kissing it softly. "Thank you." At least Ellie was joking with them, but he was concerned she'd continue to worry.

The nurse giggled, then glanced up as Max pulled up in his SUV. Logan was glad to get out of the wheelchair and climbed into the back of the SUV and thanked the nurse. As she walked back through the doors, Ellie closed his door and walked around the vehicle. She climbed into the car and settled next to Logan. Sierra sat in the front.

"All right. Logan, I'll take you home first." Max glanced at Ellie in the rearview mirror. "Ellie, Sierra and I will go get your car at your shop and drop it off at Logan's house."

"My house?" Logan looked at her.

"Yes. The doctor said you shouldn't be alone for at least twenty-four hours."

"The doctor didn't say that." Logan was curious why she was insisting on staying with him.

"He did. Don't you remember?" Ellie's eyes flared with determination.

"Ah yes, I do now." Logan did now that she reminded him. Momentary forgetfulness could be part of the concussion. He sat back. In a way, part of him was happy she was going to stay with him, but they also needed to discuss a few things once they were alone.

When his house came into view, Logan was more than ready. He was tired; his tailbone hurt, and his head was pounding. None of it was surprising, considering his injuries.

Logan winced as he climbed out of the SUV. "Did the doctor give you anything for pain?" Ellie asked.

"No, only said ibuprofen or acetaminophen if I needed it." Logan dug into his pocket for his keys.

Ellie took them and walked ahead of him to open the door. "Thanks for the ride, Max," Logan said as Max walked up to him.

"Can I bring anything back for you when I bring Ellie's car?"

Logan searched his memory. "Maybe a couple of pizzas. I haven't eaten, and I doubt Ellie has either."

"Order them from Graziano's, and I'll pick them up."

"Great." Logan reached in his pocket, and Max shook his head. Logan knew better than to argue with him.

Ellie walked back to them. "Is everything okay?"

"We're fine." Logan captured her hand. "Max is going to bring your car and some food."

She nodded. "Thank you both, again. Sierra, I'll be in touch." Ellie urged Logan forward, and Max nudged him in brotherly fashion before he climbed back into his SUV and drove off. Ellie guided Logan into his home. "Would you like to sit in the family room?"

"I want to change, but first." He turned, framed her face with his hands and brushed his lips over hers. "Now, I can order the pizza and change." He released her and pulled out his cell. Luckily, it hadn't been damaged.

"I never thought to ask, where is your gun?"

"My partner took my police belt off me at the scene before the paramedics transferred me to the hospital. It's protocol whenever possible."

Ellie nodded.

"Hi, yes, this is Logan Wolfe. I want to make a pick-up order. Two large pizzas. One meat lover's and one cheese." He glanced at Ellie, and she nodded.

"Please get the deluxe salad," she whispered.

"Yes, and a large deluxe salad. Oh, and two orders of your cheesy garlic bread. Yes, that's it. Max Preston is going to pick the order up."

Logan nodded. "Yes, just a second." He pulled his wallet out. He wasn't going to let Max pay for their food. Max and Sierra were doing enough for him and Ellie. He read off his credit card number. Max wouldn't be happy that Logan had paid. Too bad. "Twenty minutes is fine. Thank you."

"Now that food is out of the way, I'm going to go take a shower and change."

"Do you need help?"

"Sweetheart, if you help me, food will be the last thing on my mind."

Ellie's cheeks turned pink, and he chuckled as he made his way down the hall to his bedroom. Some acetaminophen and hopefully he'd be right as rain. Then after they ate and talked, they could have some fun.

Chapter 12

Logan sat back on the sofa. Max had come and gone, not without giving Logan a stern look because Logan had paid for their food. Ellie had fussed around his kitchen, getting him food and something to drink. Non-alcoholic. She'd insisted.

He didn't argue with her. Now she sat on the sofa beside him, and he put his arm around her shoulders, cuddling her to his side. "How are you doing?"

"I'm fine. It's you I'm worried about."

"That's what I wanted to talk about." He looked down at her head on his shoulder. "Look at me, please." Ellie tilted her head until their gazes met. "I'm not saying this to make you feel better. I'm doing okay. Yes, my headache has gone away, but my muscles hurt. That happens, but otherwise, nothing is wrong."

"How can you say that?" She stiffened in his arms, but Logan wasn't letting go.

"It was an accident. My partner didn't follow protocol. The suspect was able to push me, and I lost my balance. That was all."

"You hit your head on the ground?"

"Yes." He wouldn't lie to her. "I lost consciousness for a split second. It wasn't bad."

"But it could have been worse."

"Ellie, sweetheart." He moved his free hand around and gripped her chin. "If I think of all the things that could happen, I wouldn't be able to function." How could he make her understand?

"I get that."

"On the job, I don't take chances. My partner is new. My boss will sit down with him, go over the situation, and explain what he did wrong."

"Makes sense."

"Why do I feel like you're telling me what you think I want to hear?" He wanted Ellie to feel comfortable with what happened but didn't know how to make that happen.

"I don't mean to. I do understand. It was an accident, but a part of me wonders what happens if the next accident involves a knife or a gun?"

"Pleasant Valley doesn't have a large amount of crime. Yes, we have some. Usually petty things like stolen cars, some breaking and entering, and our fair share of domestic violence." She shivered in his arms. "But if we think a situation could devolve or if it does devolve, we call for back-up and wait, if possible. My boss and the higher ups believe in keeping their officers safe. I could as easily be hurt driving to work or driving to the club."

"In here"—she tapped her head—"I know that. In here"—she patted her chest where her heart was—"worry lives."

"I want to ease that worry, but I don't know how." How had his mother survived this? Yes, he'd been in his twenties when his father died, but his father had been a police officer before Logan was born. Maybe he should have a chat with his mother and see if she had any tips.

"I don't either. But for today, I know you're okay. You're alive and with me. I have to hold onto that."

"Why don't I show you?" He shifted to stand, a wide grin on his face.

Ellie shook her head. "You need to rest. We have time."

Logan settled back and nodded, believing they did have time, and only time would help Ellie see.

* * * *

Ellie glanced up at Logan's relaxed face. He'd fallen asleep a little bit ago. She snuggled closer to him, her hand over his chest. The feel of his heartbeat settled her nerves. What she'd said to Logan earlier was so true. Her mind understood today was just a freak accident, but her heart feared him dying and leaving her forever.

In a short time, Logan had become important to her. She'd cared about her ex, at first, but not like this. Logan was different. She couldn't put her finger on it. Ellie didn't want to walk away from him or what she'd found with him, but was she being selfish in wanting to stay in his life when there was a possibility she wouldn't be able to handle him being hurt?

Maybe they shouldn't see each other too much out of the club, not that they had. Well, there had been dinners here and there, but Logan worked a lot, and when he was off on weekends, they went to the club.

She sighed and closed her eyes. There were no easy answers here, but one thing Logan was right about: They needed to communicate, and that meant when she was scared. She needed to tell him. Except she'd never been very good about sharing her fears.

* * * *

Ellie woke slowly the next morning, stretching before she opened her eyes. She'd slept really well last night, considering… Logan. Ellie sat up. She was in Logan's bed. How did that happen? Last thing she remembered was closing her eyes while they cuddled on his sofa.

"Morning, sweetheart," Logan said, strolling into the bedroom with a mug in his hand. Her mouth watered. He wore a pair of low riding sweats and a sleeveless t-shirt.

"Morning. How did I get here?" And…okay she was in her bra and panties. So Logan must have undressed her. Her body heated.

"I carried you." He handed her the mug.

The scent of fresh brewed coffee hit her senses. She blew on the brew before taking a sip. A moan slipped past her lips as she sipped the wonderful nectar, then she processed his words. "Carried me? Logan, you could have hurt yourself."

He chuckled and sat on the mattress, his hip brushing her thigh beneath the sheet. "You're not heavy, and I feel great."

"No headaches, nausea, or anything?" she asked, keeping her gaze on him.

"Nothing. A twinge of a muscle here and there, but nothing major." He brushed her cheek. "What would you like for breakfast?"

"I can cook for you." His features were relaxed, and nothing about him looked injured. Ellie took another sip of her coffee, trying to process her feelings about him looking after her when he was the one who was hurt.

Logan stared at her. "Not going to happen. Eggs, bacon, and toast good?"

"You don't have to cook." Ellie shifted. How could she make him understand she didn't need him to do this?

"Stop squirming." His voice grew husky. "Yesterday gave you a scare, and I'm sorry for that. You barely ate last night, and I'm sure you're hungry this morning."

He was right. She'd only eaten a small amount of salad and a piece of pizza. She'd been so worried about him. Now, her stomach was demanding food.

"See." He rubbed her tummy. "Finish your coffee. There are amenities in the bathroom for you, along with my robe." He stood.

"Thanks."

Logan left the room, and Ellie climbed out of bed. She didn't like the idea of wearing her underwear for another day, but what choice did she have. Her clothes from yesterday were lying folded up on a chair, she grabbed them and padded into the bathroom.

Amenities, my ass. He'd laid out a toothbrush, toothpaste, brush and comb, washcloth and a fresh towel. Ellie shook her head. She quickly brushed her teeth and cleaned up. Shaking her clothes out, she frowned.

She'd ask Logan if she could run her clothes through the washer and dryer. That would make her feel better. But what could she use for underwear?

Slipping on his robe, she threw her clothes over one arm and strolled into the bedroom. "Logan," she called.

"Yes."

How did one ask for what she needed? "Ummm. Can I borrow a pair of your underwear?" Heat invaded her face.

"Second drawer. Take your pick."

He didn't even hesitate. What did that mean? She decided to analyze it later. Setting her clothes on the chair, she found a pair of boxers and slipped them on under the robe. Of course, they were a little baggy, but they would work. She didn't feel comfortable going commando.

Gathering up her clothes once again and picking up her empty mug, she made her way toward the kitchen. She stopped when she passed the utility room.

"I'm going to throw my clothes in the washer, okay?"

"Sure. Detergent on the shelf above the dryer."

Ellie made quick work of it and then walked into the kitchen. Logan's back was to her as he cooked. "Should only be a few minutes before breakfast is ready."

"Thanks. Can I do anything?"

"Pour more coffee, at least for me, and have a seat at the table."

Ellie moved to the coffee pot, poured herself another cup and then filled Logan's before carrying them to the table. She sat so she could face him.

"Are you off work today?"

He glanced over at her, then back at the food. "Yes. Boss left me a voicemail. I'm off until next Monday."

"Good."

"Oh, really?" He turned off the burner, covered the food with lids, turned, and stalked toward her.

Ellie swallowed at the look of determination on his face. "You need to rest."

"I need to remind you who is dominant in this relationship."

She blinked. "Just because you're dominant eighty percent of the time doesn't mean I'm wrong." She pushed her chair back as he continued his predatory trek toward her.

"Eighty percent?" He leaned over her and put his hands on the back of the chair, trapping her.

"Even you need time off." The heat coming off his body enveloped hers. Had she poked the bear a little too hard?

"That doesn't mean I'm not your Dom."

"That's not what I said."

His eyebrows rose.

Ellie could barely breathe. Her body was reacting to Logan's actions. He was in Dom mode, and her body loved it, and if she was honest, she did too.

"Explain what you meant, then."

"What I meant was you can't always be dominant on the job or in life."

"You think there's an off switch?"

"I don't know about an off switch, but I think you would get tired after a while. You need to relax and rest, too, without worrying about anyone else. You need to let go now and then. And remember: You promised me autonomy on some decisions."

He continued to stare at her, and Ellie didn't know what else to say.

"That's very insightful of you." He straightened and made his way into the kitchen where he dished up their food and brought the plates over to the table. He placed her plate in front of her, then sat across from her with his. "I think today we should talk more about how our D/s relationship is going to continue."

"D/s?" She hadn't heard that acronym yet.

"Dominant/submissive."

"I'd like that. Logan, I'm afraid I'll lose myself in this relationship. I lost myself once before. I won't do that again."

"I won't let you lose yourself." He reached over and placed his hand over hers. "We're partners in this."

"We are? Even when I get scared?"

"Especially then. I want you to feel free to speak your mind. Relationships are always better with open and honest communication."

"I won't argue with that." She couldn't because he was right. She picked up a piece of bacon with her free hand and nibbled on it.

"Eat. We both need fuel." He withdrew his hand, and she missed his touch.

Ellie nodded. The eggs were light and fluffy, the bacon crisp, and even the toast was the right color on both sides. Was there anything this man couldn't do?

* * * *

Logan forced himself not to smile as he ate. Ellie wasn't afraid to take him on. He made her nervous, especially when he was standing over her, but most women would be. Still, she held her ground, and he admired her for it.

They needed to discuss their relationship, both in and out of the club. "Don't you need to go to work today?" he asked.

"I'm fine. I don't have any appointments, and my landline is forwarded to my cell." The washer buzzer went off. Ellie jumped up and disappeared, then returned. "I put the clothes in the dryer."

He nodded and continued eating, while in his head he sought a way for Ellie to take the week off and spend it with him. Would she do that? He wasn't sure. It would be great if they could spend more time together.

He realized how comfortable he was with Ellie around. The only people he'd ever cooked for were his mother, brother, and sister.

Ellie fit in his domain. She wasn't telling him how he could change things, making the room more feminine or anything like that. The hadn't know each other that long, but they worked together quite well, and that wasn't something he was ready to give up on. He hoped he was enhancing her life as well.

Logan polished off his food and waited for Ellie to finish. When she was done, he took their plates to the sink and made quick work of cleaning everything up. The dryer stopped, and Ellie stood.

"Time to get dressed."

"I like you in my robe." She looked adorable in his black robe, and he wanted to see her in it more often.

She ducked her head. "Thanks. Be right back."

God, he loved it when she blushed like that. He'd spend his life making sure she knew how sexy and beautiful she was.

While she was gone, he pulled a couple of steaks out of the freezer and set them out to defrost, then went to the pantry. He had a couple of potatoes, and if he remembered correctly, he had some veggies in the fridge.

Grilled steaks and veggie stuffed potatoes would make a good dinner. Dessert? He rubbed his chin and checked his pantry shelves. Not much. He wasn't a big baker, but he found a pre-made graham cracker pie crust, and a couple boxes of chocolate pudding. He set them on the counter.

Back at the freezer, he grabbed a tub of whipped topping and then opened the fridge. Yep, he had milk. That would make a great chocolate cream pie. Dinner and desert taken care of. Lunch could be left over salad and pizza from last night.

Ellie strolled back into the room. Her expression was closed down, and he was pretty sure that wasn't a good thing. What had she been thinking while she got dressed? "I should get home."

"Why?" He walked over to her and took her hand in his. "Spend the day with me."

"Shouldn't you rest?"

"I can rest with you here. Besides, this would be a good time for us to talk about our relationship."

"I really would like to run home, shower, and change at least."

He couldn't argue with her on that. "I'll drive you."

"My car is here. I can drive myself."

"Yes, you can, but I want to drive you. Will you let me take care of you, like you took care of me last night?"

"I really didn't do anything."

"You greeted Max when he arrived with your car and food. Gave me food, then cleaned up after dinner. And you snuggled with me as we watched TV. You were here if I needed you, and I liked it."

"I liked it too," she said softly.

"Please."

"All right you can come with me, but I'm driving."

He was happy she'd allowed him to do this, but still confused as hell about her change in attitude. "Let me grab a shirt and shoes, then we can go."

She nodded. "My shoes are by the front door."

Logan ran to his bedroom. He grabbed a polo shirt and pulled it over his head, slipped on a pair of socks then grabbed his loafers. Probably took him less than five minutes before he joined Ellie at the front door. She was toying with the zipper on her purse.

"Am I pushing you too hard?" He was aware he could push too fast, too hard with people.

She shook her head. "I'm just thinking."

"Should I be worried?" He reached around her, unlocked the door, and held it open to her.

"No." She pushed past him and headed down the walkway.

His worry shot up. What was there to think about? He would have to watch his step with Ellie, or he might find himself in trouble. He slid into the passenger seat of her car and pondered the questions flowing through his brain.

* * * *

Ellie was quiet as Logan went with her to her place. He let her drive, which surprised her. Once inside her apartment, she made sure he was comfortable on the sofa, then she escaped into her bedroom.

In the shower, she let her tears fall. She'd been holding them in all morning. Logan was upset by her tears, and the last thing she wanted to do was hurt him. Luckily for her, she wasn't a noisy crier.

After she cried herself out, she finished her shower and got dressed. She did feel better, having had a good cry, except now she was tired. Crying always did that to her. Logan mentioned he wanted to talk about their relationship, but was she ready for that?

Stepping out of the bedroom, she gazed at him sitting on her sofa. Her heart pounded. This man had come to mean so much to her so quickly, and it was scary. Logan turned his head and grinned.

"Can I convince you to pack a bag and stay at my place for tonight at least?"

Ellie stood there. Her heart screamed yes, but her head told her to slow down. Except her heart won out. She'd sorted her emotions out in the shower.

"I think you might."

His grin widened, and his eyes lit up.

At that moment, all felt right in Ellie's world. "Give me an hour."

"Go. I'm happy right here."

* * * *

They returned to his house almost two hours from the time they left. While Ellie packed, he hung out in her living room, browsing her bookshelves and getting to understand her more. Logan was surprised she'd agreed to at least spend the night at his house. He wasn't going to push for more.

The day was sunny and warm, so instead of having their chat inside, he suggested they talk on the patio. Once she settled in one of the chairs, he grabbed another chair and sat in front of her.

His knees brushed hers.

"Aren't you sitting a little close?"

"No. I want to be close." He reached over and took her hands in his. "I like being close to you, touching you."

"I've noticed."

"Does it bother you?"

"I wouldn't say it bothers me. It's something to get used to. Most people I know are not so touchy/feely."

"Well, I am, and I'm pretty sure most of the women at the club are as well."

Ellie laughed, and his heart lightened. She was back to being Ellie, not the silent Ellie. "Yeah, they are."

"Shall we discuss us?"

"I guess. I'm not very good at these types of discussions."

Her response wasn't enthusiastic, but that wasn't going to stop him. "Communication is important, and I want to keep the lines open between us. Not only about our time in the club, but outside it as well."

"I understand. I'm just not sure what we have to talk about."

"How do you feel about us being together more outside the club?" He wasn't going to beat around the bush.

"Depends on what you mean."

"Dinners, spending nights in my bed."

"You're bed? What about mine?"

"I'm game if you want me to be in your bed."

"Your work hours don't make some of that easy."

She was right. "Agreed, but I can ask about going to a normal eight hours a day, five days a week with weekends off."

"Can you do that?"

"Yes. I was able to make sure I had weekends off for us to go to the club. I'm not saying there won't be times when I have to work late or work a weekend, but I've been with the department long enough they'll agree to what I want."

"I'm still not sure we should dive into something serious right now."

"Is it because of what happened to me?"

"Partially. Logan, your job is dangerous, no matter what you say."

"I won't argue the point. It can be dangerous." He took a deep breath. "There hasn't been a death to an officer on duty in about fifteen years. While Pleasant Valley isn't so large you don't know your neighbors, it's not so small you know everyone in town. Yet it is a place where everyone looks out for everyone else."

"Can we take this slow?"

At least she wasn't totally resistant to the idea. "We can. Tell me what your version of slow is?"

"Dinner once a week, and on club nights, we can spend the night together."

For him, it wasn't ideal, but for Ellie, he'd try and do what she asked. "I can live with that."

Her features softened.

"Do you have to work the rest of this week?" he asked.

"I do. Tomorrow, I have meetings with vendors, and Thursday, two clients are coming in."

"Friday?"

"I can take Friday off."

"Let's start there. Now on to our D/s relationship." Her hands jerked in his. "How would you feel if we start doing more in the club?"

"Like?"

"Would you be willing to scene with your top off?" Nudity had been on her soft limit list. He'd take it step at a time.

"Only in the scene. I wouldn't have to walk around the club topless, would I?"

"Only if you want to." While he'd love to have her breasts free in the club, he would let her decide. It would take her time to feel comfortable.

"I think I can do it in a scene."

Logan nodded. "How would you feel about more bondage and flogging?" He was sticking with soft limits he wanted to push.

"Explain more to me, please."

"We've been using the bondage chair. I'd like to use the St. Andrew's Cross, which would mean flogging your back and legs. Also using one of the bondage horses. The bondage part would be different on the horse."

"What kind of flogger?"

"We'd start with a rabbit flogger, move to a suede, and only go to heavier floggers when you're ready."

"I think I can handle that."

"I want to remind you: You can say your safe word at any time."

She smiled. "I remember."

"Last thing I want to discuss: How do you feel about playing here at my house or at your apartment?"

Her eyes widened. "Outside the club?"

"Yes. I'm not talking more than you're ready to give. Some bondage and flogging, but also toys, full nudity."

Her eyes widened. "I hadn't thought about that."

He kept his gaze on her, giving her time to think. Ellie tilted her head, but her features were closed down, and Logan couldn't figure out what she was thinking. Unusual for him, because he was good at reading people.

"What happens if I can't play outside the club?" Her voice soft.

"Then we play in the club only and keep the bedroom for making love." He could do that. D/s wasn't the end-all be-all for him. He liked playing with Ellie in the club, and while he wanted to do more privately, she had to be comfortable with it.

"I'd like to try. But please understand I might call my safe word more often than in the club."

"Why would that be?" What did she think he was going to do?

"You know this is new to me."

"Yes."

"I'm not very good with relationships. I don't know if you've noticed, but I have trouble letting go of my control."

Logan pondered her words. "I've not been in a long-term relationship." What could he say to make her more comfortable. "You seem to let go of your control with me."

"In the club, yes."

"You weren't in control the other night in my bed." He understood how hard it was to let go of one's control. When he was mentored as a Dom, one of the things he had to learn was letting his own control go and rely on the Dom teaching him. It hadn't been easy, but it gave him a better understanding of submission.

"No, I wasn't." There was surprise on her face. "I hadn't thought about it like that."

"I promise to do my best to make you comfortable and happy. I won't violate hard limits. I might push the soft ones a bit, but I will always stop if you use your safe word."

Her features softened. "I'm willing to try." She smiled. "When do we start?"

"Now." His fingers itched to have her soft, creamy skin under them again. His cock pulsed with anticipation.

"Logan." She shook her head. "You still need to recover from yesterday. I haven't missed the way you wince when you get up after sitting too long."

Ellie was too observant. While he didn't want to admit weakness, his body was telling him to take it easy. "All right. Why don't we watch a movie or something?" No reason they couldn't touch while they were watching a movie.

"Oh, you don't fool me." There was laughter in her voice. This woman could switch moods on a dime. He'd have to watch her more carefully. "We can watch a movie, but no hanky-panky."

Damn, she was calling him out. "All right, but I get to cuddle you."

"Cuddling is permissible."

"Fine. But on Friday, you're mine."

"Agreed."

Logan stood and pulled her from her chair. He drew her into his arms and brushed his lips against hers. "Is that against your rules?"

"As long as it's only kissing."

"Kissing is fun." He tugged her inside and gestured to the sofa while he found his remote. Finding the streaming service, he pulled up the menu. "What would you like to watch?"

"Why don't you pick."

Her words surprised him, but he was going to go with the flow. He found an action-adventure movie and started it. After setting the remote aside, he pulled Ellie into his arms. Her head rested on his shoulder. She fit perfectly against his body, and Logan didn't mind that they were doing nothing but sitting together. He liked having her here with him.

* * * *

Two hours later, the movie ended. Ellie reached over, pushed the button on the remote and turned the TV off. Logan had fallen asleep less than an hour into the movie. She'd been content to lay in his arms while he slept.

After crying in the shower and letting her mind settle, she was feeling better. His proposition about them playing outside the club had thrown her. She hadn't expected their kink to spill outside the club. She had no idea why she thought that, because a lot of the people in the club were couples outside of it.

Why was she being so snappish about this? She wanted to be with him and not have to be in control, right? Yes. It was one of the reasons she'd sought out the club in the first place.

Logan was caring and careful. He always made sure she was comfortable, even if their conversation was a bit uncomfortable. She didn't mind him pushing for answers. She learned new things about herself every time.

While she didn't like the vulnerable feeling being restrained gave her, it also gave her permission to let go. It helped her realize she didn't need to take on the entire world herself. Logan did that for her. Helped her let go of that responsibility.

They fit. That was how she thought of it. She'd never pictured herself with a man in law enforcement, especially after her brother's death. But Logan seemed to understand her fear of him being hurt or killed on the job.

There was responsibility raising its ugly head once again. Logan was a grown man and had a good grasp of the dangers of his job. Was she learning to accept it? In a way. She would always worry. It would never go away, but she also trusted Logan to be safe.

In a way, that's what it came down to. Trust. She trusted Logan. Her brother thought he was invincible. Logan didn't think that way, at least not that she'd seen. He was down to earth. Ellie closed her eyes and listened to his even breathing.

Her breath caught in her throat. Logan meant something to her. Allowing herself to get close to anyone was a feeling she'd shut down a long time ago.

But lately she'd been dissatisfied with her life.

She had enough help with her business, so that wasn't why. And she had good friends. And now she had Logan. Maybe it was time to let him fully into her life.

"You're not asleep. I can hear you thinking."

"I'm relaxing."

His arms tightened around her. "Cuddle against me. I like having you in my arms."

"I can tell." She snuggled closer as she pushed all thoughts about anyone other than Logan out of her mind. It was time for her to live her life, her way, with a man who understood her.

Logan's stomach growled. "Hungry?" It had been around noon when they started the movie.

"A bit."

"Let me get us some food." She sat up.

"There's leftover pizza and salad in the fridge. That will work." He sat up and rubbed his arm. "I have a steaks defrosting for dinner."

"I'm not very good at cooking steak. I have a tendency to burn them."

"I have a very nice grill I can cook on." Ellie stared at him, and he put his hands up. "Grilling isn't going to hurt me." His stomach growled louder. "Pizza. Now, woman."

She put her hands on her hips and glared at him. "Keep talking like that, and I'll feed you liver."

He grimaced. "Sorry, my brain doesn't work well when I'm hungry."

Ellie laughed and sauntered into the kitchen, knowing she'd made the right decision. Logan was good for her.

Chapter 13

Ellie rubbed her back as she straightened from packing up all the Halloween decorations, in her shop, for the party this Saturday at Wicked Sanctuary. She grinned as she remembered Max's disgruntled look when Sierra informed him that they were taking over the club Saturday morning to transform it without him there to oversee.

Max obviously hadn't liked the idea, but Sierra had a way of making him agree. Ellie's vendors were lined up to bring the equipment they needed, with non-disclosure agreements in place. It was something Max insisted on, and Ellie understood.

Ellie plopped into her office chair and glanced at her computer calendar. She'd cleared it for this week. What parties there were, her people would take care of them. For the next few days, all her focus was on the club and Logan.

The past few weeks with Logan had cemented her decision to keep him in her life. While they played in the club on Friday and Saturday nights, during the week, they had dinner and spent their nights together. Not every night, but several nights, especially Friday night and Saturdays.

The bell over the door jangled, and Ellie walked out of her office and into the main room.

"Ladies." The whole sub group from the club walked into her shop looking decidedly worried.

"We have a problem," Sierra said.

"Oh no. What's the issue? Did Max veto something?" Ellie hoped not. This was going to be an epic Halloween party.

"He wouldn't dare," Crystal said.

"Nothing like that." Sierra waved her hands to encompass the group. "We need costumes."

"Oh. How could I forget." Ellie grabbed her cell. "I made notes on costumes and sizes that night when we discussed it in the club. But totally forgot to order them." She glanced over her notes. It was so unlike her to forget things, but with everything with Logan, that part slipped her mind. "What about the dress code?" Some of the ideas were unusual, well maybe not, considering this group.

"It's a little more relaxed when we have private parties," Tessa said.

"Okay. Give me a minute to make a phone call." This close to Halloween, there was only one person who could get things done for her.

* * * *

"What do you think those women are up to?" Max asked Logan a few days later.

"You're asking me?" Logan sat back in his chair, holding a mug of coffee. He'd met Max and some of the other Doms at Sweet & Savory this morning.

"Didn't Ellie say anything?" Jordan asked.

"Not a word. She's been pretty close-mouthed about the party tonight." Logan couldn't believe how fast the past few weeks had gone. Hell, he could hardly believe how great they'd been. He'd spent a lot of time with Ellie.

He'd been able to change his shifts to a straight day shift. It took him a week to get used to the routine, but he was happier and so was Ellie. Their club and home play had advanced as well.

"Tessa won't say anything, either, only that we're in for a surprise," Damon said.

"At least Ralph is there while they set up," Max muttered. "I hate surprises."

"You'll like this one," Lara commented as she refilled their coffee cups.

"What do you know?" Max stared at Lara.

Lara shook her head and walked away.

"She's catering the party tonight, isn't she?" Logan asked.

"Yes. Colby is going to help her, but he told me that they wouldn't get there until about six-thirty, so he has no idea either," Max said.

"They're going to cut it close to the club opening," Jordan commented.

Max nodded and looked at his watch. "Well, looks like whatever Ellie is having delivered has arrived. I just got an alert that the gate opened."

"When did you put that on your watch?" Damon asked.

"When my wife decided that she wanted to throw this party and refused to let me be there while they set up."

Logan watched Max. While his tone was somewhat sharp, Logan could see the curiosity on his face. What were the women up to? "How dangerous can the subs be?" he asked.

Three pairs of eyes zeroed in on him. "You have no idea," Damon said.

"Who has no idea?" Zeke asked as he and Gabriel grabbed chairs and joined them.

"Logan, about how devious our subs can be," Jordan said.

The men groaned.

"Allyson and Dani have been secretive as well," Zeke said.

"The women have ganged up on us," Gabriel mumbled.

"When don't they?" Damon threw his hands up in the air.

"Coffee?" Lara asked.

"Yes, please," Zeke and Gabriel replied.

She poured them coffee. "If you want food, just holler."

"Lara, what is going on at the club?" Gabriel asked.

"A surprise." She glared at Max. "Don't give me that stare. For once in your lives, you guys need to just be patient." Lara left, and the men shook their heads.

"I guess we're stuck waiting," Logan said.

"I hate waiting." Max grumbled.

* * * *

"Frankenstein over there." Ellie pointed to the area between the St. Andrew's Cross and a spanking bench. The women had worked, with Ralph's help, as fast as they could to cover the equipment before her vendors arrived.

While they had signed NDAs, Ellie felt covering the equipment would be better. Ralph was also keeping a sharp eye on the delivery personnel to make sure they didn't wander off.

"Where do you want this one, Ellie?" one of the men asked.

"Over there." She was damn near shaking with excitement. This was going to be fun. Almost all of the subs had shown up at nine to help. They waited by the bar while the men brought in the items she'd ordered. They would be back to pick the items up on Monday.

Ellie glanced at Ralph. "Are you okay watching the workers while we decorate the garden."

"I can handle it." Ralph grinned at her.

"Hey, Ellie," one of the workers called.

"Yes, Greg."

"In order for us to get the dancing poles stable, we're going to need to secure them to the ceiling and floor."

"Damn, I was afraid of that." Ellie looked at Ralph.

"Ceiling is fine, but not the floor. It's specialized."

Ellie looked at the area, then back to Ralph. "Can we remove the flooring?" The floor was soft and spongy.

Ralph frowned at her as Sierra came up. "We can," Sierra said.

"Miss Sierra, I can't be responsible for that."

Sierra waved her hand at Ralph. "I'll take responsibility. Come on Ellie, I'll show the workers what they can do. It's easy enough to replace it after the party."

"Thanks for your help, Ralph," Ellie said, then followed Sierra.

After Sierra explained how to remove a square of floor covering, the guys assured her they would make sure to put it back around the poles so everything looked right. Ellie and Sierra then walked over to the bar where the other subs sat.

"Max is going to be upset that we've cut holes in the flooring to make it fit around the poles," Crystal said.

"Maybe. He has extra sections in storage, so it's easily replaced. But I have a feeling those poles are going to stay." She grinned.

Ellie shook her head. "Do you ladies want to start on the garden while the rest of this is set up, then we can decorate in here."

"Sounds like a plan," Sierra, said and the group trooped out to the garden carrying the bags of decorations Ellie had stashed in the women's room yesterday. There was so much stuff, but in order for this to work, they had to have a lot.

Thankfully, the weather had held. An unusual warmth for October and it wasn't going away. Today would be in the mid 70s. For some, that wasn't hot, but here in the Pacific Northwest it was a heatwave this time of year.

An hour later, the last vendor had left, and Ellie checked all the equipment they'd brought. She made sure those that needed plugging in were secured with tape so no one would trip over them. They wouldn't plug them in until just before the doors opened.

Several of the subs came in from the garden, laughing. "Oh, my goodness, Ellie." Rose could barely talk from laughing so hard. "Those decorations. They guys are going to go nuts."

"Just wait until we do the inside. Let's get the equipment uncovered and get to work."

"Do we get to see the special items?" Regina asked with a gleam in her eyes.

"Later." The rest of the women returned from the garden.

"Ladies." Ellie clapped her hands together. "Before I forget, all the costumes are in the women's room. So you can dress later."

Excitement ran through the room.

Ellie grinned. "Let's finish decorating this place."

* * * *

"You're bouncing," Logan said to Ellie as he drove them to the club.

"Hard not to. I can't wait to see Max's reaction."

"You think he hasn't seen inside the club yet?" Logan couldn't see Max waiting.

"He hasn't. Sierra told him if he went into the club, she wouldn't have sex with him for a month."

Logan groaned. "You women know where to hit."

"Yes, we do. Don't forget it."

He enjoyed hearing the laughter in Ellie's voice. She was so much more relaxed around him and the people in the club. While she hadn't been totally comfortable removing her clothing yet, she'd allowed him to lower her bra to play with her breasts and promised to think about wearing a thong. She'd come a long way in a short time.

"Do we all get to see it at the same time?" he asked.

"Probably. The subs are arriving at six-thirty to help Lara set up, and we said the doors would open at eight for the party."

"I thought it was seven-thirty. It's bad enough we have to wait with Max at his house."

Ellie flashed him a grin. "We told you guys seven-thirty, but all the others who RSVP'd for the special members-only party were told eight. We wanted to give Max time to chill out."

"What did you do?"

"Nothing but some decorating."

"Why do I have a feeling this is going to be interesting?"

"It will be."

* * * *

At seven-twenty, the subs went into the club after changing before the men arrived from Max's house. Mostly thanks to Ralph. He'd been a godsend. Ellie smoothed her hands over her barely there black skirt. A fake police badge was secured to the waistband.

The other women were dressed in their costumes. Well, if you could call them that. Ellie wondered how Logan would react to her costume. She wanted something that reflected both of them, so her bra was black with multicolored balloons all over it. That had been an accidental find at an online lingerie company.

"Are we ready?" Ellie asked loudly over the excited voices of the subs.

"Food is ready," Lara said.

"We're all set up," Sierra said.

"Music when you're ready," Kaley called out from behind the bar.

"All right. Who is opening the doors?" Ellie asked. She could hear the Doms outside the doors.

"I will," Sierra said.

"We will," Crystal and Tessa piped up.

The three women marched up to the doors together. Ellie nodded at Kaley, and the music started.

"Lights," Ellie said. The overhead lights dimmed, and the multicolored lights started flickering. Drawing in a deep breath, Ellie stood with the other subs, her heart pounding.

* * * *

The doors to the club were opened from the inside. Logan stood with the other Doms. He immediately noticed the lighting in the club was dimmer.

"Welcome to Wicked Sanctuary."

Logan realized the woman wearing the long, figure-hugging black dress with a very deep vee in the neckline with long black hair was Sierra. "I'm your host – Miss Sierra. Please enter at your own risk."

"Damn," someone whispered.

"I'm a dead man," another voice said.

"Miss Sierra, I am Master Max; it would be my pleasure to be your escort tonight." Max stepped forward and held his hand out to her.

Logan almost laughed at the wide grin on Max's face when he saw his sub. The man had been pacing and grumbling only two minutes earlier.

"Master Max, how appropriate. I accept. But please, everyone come in. There are delights for all."

The men flowed in, and Logan searched for Ellie. Jordan grabbed Crystal by the waist, as she was dressed as a naughty paralegal. Then there was Tessa, who played the naughty librarian, telling Damon he needed a library card to touch her.

When Logan found Ellie, his mouth dropped open. "Fuck me," he whispered as he walked up to her. The short skirt barely covered her assets, and the bra with the balloons on it caused him to grin. And something else perked up too.

"Evening, Officer," her voice was soft and quiet as the music played in the background.

Squeals could be heard as the other Doms found their partners. Logan only had eyes for Ellie. "You look…" He was at a loss for words.

"I hope you like it." There was a small tremor in her voice.

"I love it." Logan took her hand and lifted it to his lips, before he swept her into his arms. "You are fucking gorgeous." His slid his hands down to her ass and beneath the skirt. Skin met skin. His eyes widened. "The outfit is wonderful." He squeezed her ass.

"Easy, Sir."

"What do you have on?" he whispered.

"A thong, just for you, Sir."

His dick hardened, and Logan shifted on his feet.

"Look around Sir," she said.

He reluctantly forced his gaze from Ellie's face to the club. When he saw the decorations and other things, his jaw dropped open.

"Max seems to be okay with what we did, at least I hope so, Sir." Her voice was tentative.

Logan took in the spiderwebs around the equipment, and what was in the webs?

"You put toys in the webs?" He shook his head.

"Yes, what else would spiders collect in a BDSM club, Sir."

The sparkling lights gave the club a different look. Then he heard the cackling of witch, the moan of a ghost, and the rattling of chains. He turned his attention to the two poles on the right side of the room, and his eyebrows rose. Stripper poles. Interesting.

Then he saw the big Frankenstein sitting in the corner, and someone screamed. Logan turned his head to see Dracula reaching from his coffin with a huge dildo between his legs. "How did you do all this?"

"I have connections, Sir."

"I see." He looked down at her. "Who is arresting whom tonight?" He spied the fake badge on her skirt.

"Oh I don't know, Sir. I'm a rookie, and you'll have to train me."

The laughter in her voice made him grin. "Oh, I'll train you," he said with a devious chuckle. "Okay rookie, as the senior officer, you will do exactly as you are told tonight. Is that clear?"

"Yes, Sir." She gave him a salute.

The music volume was lowered, and Max stood on one of the stages. "Everyone, before the rest of the group gets here, I want to thank Ellie and her helpers for this wonderful party."

Applause swelled.

"Food is available; the bar is open—non-acholic drinks, of course. Feel free to use any of the equipment, just be careful of the spiderwebs. I've been told they're sticky. I've also been informed there will be a big surprise in the garden at one a.m.." Max glanced at Sierra standing next to him. "The Mistress of the Dark here will let us know when we can go out there. For now, it's off limits. Relax and enjoy these spectacular, umm, decorations." He finished by pulling Sierra into his arms for a sweltering kiss, dipping her low over his arm and kissing skin at the bottom of the vee in her dress.

The music came back on, and the couples mingled while the unattached subs gathered in the green area. There would be unattached Doms here tonight, so everyone would have a good time.

"Where should we play first?" Logan asked.

"Wherever you wish, Sir."

Logan eyed the bondage system. It had some decorations, but these wouldn't interfere with what he wanted to do. "Go to the bondage station and wait for me."

"Yes, Sir." Ellie turned and walked away, shaking her ass at him.

"Watch yourself," he yelled, and she shook her ass harder.

Logan moved to the bar area and pulled his bag out of his cubby. "I think the women surprised us," Anthony remarked as he pulled his own bag out.

"They certainly did. I didn't see Kaley."

"In the poodle skirt." Anthony pointed across the room where Kaley stood by the spanking benches.

"Ah." Logan noticed how the women pretty much wore costumes around their individual jobs outside the club, except Sierra. "Later." He turned and made his way to where Ellie stood. She was eyeing the bondage system.

Logan dropped his bag on the stage and took Ellie's hand and led her over to the single chair. He sat down and pulled her into his lap.

"Remind me what you are wearing under your skirt?" he asked as he ran his fingers over her skin.

"A thong, Sir."

"How do you feel about losing the bra and skirt?" It was a new step for them in the club. Ellie swallowed, her gaze on him.

"I'm willing to try, Sir." While her voice was soft, there was a breathless quality to it.

"Thank you." He kept is touch light. "We haven't been on this stage yet. What questions do you have?"

"A million, Sir." She flashed him a grin.

"Ask away."

Ellie bit her lower lip, and it took all of Logan's control not to kiss her silly. He wanted her to be comfortable with what they did tonight.

"What are you planning to do, Sir?" She turned her head and glanced at the bondage system.

"I want to restrain your arms to the crossbar, then your legs to the slats. They will be spread." Like the bondage chair, the legs were wide open.

"Okay, Sir."

"Then I want to tease you and play with your breasts. Maybe some nipple clamps. I want you to experience being semi-nude in the club."

She took a deep breath and let it out. "Sounds good, Sir."

"Plus some light flogging." He paused, but she didn't say anything. "Oh, there will be kissing and touching, wherever I choose." Her eyes grew wide, and a blush started in her chest and rose to her face. "Are you okay with that?"

Ellie nodded.

"Words. Ellie. I need consent."

"Yes, Sir. I'm okay with it."

"Thank you, sweetheart." He kissed her temple. "If you feel uncomfortable, you have your safe words."

"I do, Sir." She took a deep breath.

Logan had a feeling she was holding something back. "Ellie." He framed her cheeks with his palms and gazed into her eyes. "Am I pushing too hard?"

"No, Sir." Her breath shuddered in and out. "Am I a bit uncomfortable? Yes. But I do want to try."

"Okay." He didn't blame her for feelings. He was pushing her out of her comfort zone. "Stand up."

Ellie stood and took two steps away as Logan stood. "I'll let you undress as I get the bondage system and my toys ready."

Logan left Ellie standing by the chair while he set things up. When he turned to her, she was standing close to him in her thong and bra.

"Sir, if you could remove my bra once I'm seated and restrained, I would appreciate it."

"I can do that."

Ellie took her seat on the bondage system. Logan kept his gaze on her. Her breathing was a little fast, but he didn't see any hesitation in her features, and her eyes gleamed with anticipation. "I'm going to do your legs first."

"Yes, Sir."

He put the restraints on her ankles and then her upper thighs. She squirmed a bit as her legs were spread wide, but nothing else.

"Slip your arms out of your bra please."

She did as he asked, though the fabric clung to her breasts. He then restrained her arms. Standing between her legs, he unfastened her bra. Her swift intake of breath made him hesitate. "Ellie?"

"I'm okay, Sir."

Her skin was flushed. Logan stepped back and placed her bra on the chair where her skirt lay. Then he picked up the feather tickler and began running it over her skin.

* * * *

Ellie could barely breathe after Logan took off her bra. She was exposed to everyone in the club. A quick glance around and she realized no one was paying attention to them. Many were doing their own scenes or having fun with the props she'd arranged.

She could do this. Someone seeing her breasts wasn't different in the club. Heck, probably about half the women were topless by now—or darn close. Something tickled her skin and brought her out of her thoughts.

Logan ran a feather over her skin, causing her to shiver at the sensation. It wasn't unpleasant, and it tickled at times. He trailed the feather over her nipples, and her buds stiffened.

"How are you doing?"

"Green, Sir." She loved how he often checked in on her. No matter where they played, inside or outside the club, he continually made sure she was comfortable. It was comforting and sexy.

184

"Those nipples are nice and pink; I think they need some attention." Ellie watched him set the feather down and pick up a pair of tweezer looking things. "These are tweezer clamps for your nipples."

Ellie sucked in a breath as he applied the first one, adjusting the tension until she bit her lip, then he moved to her other nipple. The tingling in her nipples made her shiver. Her clit was beginning to throb. They'd played with nipple clamps at home but never in the club.

"I have something special to go with those clamps." He dangled two pieces of teardrop jewelry in front of her.

"Sir?" What was he planning?

"I'm going to attach one to the bottom of each clamp, like this." He opened the clasp, hooked it into the small opening at the end of the tweezer clamp, and then released it.

Ellie's mouth fell open on a moan. The extra weight… She couldn't describe it. It didn't hurt, but it made her very aware of her nipples. Then he did the same with the left nipple.

"How are we doing?"

"Green, Sir." Those little pieces of jewelry upped her body temperature. She was hot and bothered. That was a mild way to put it. Pure desire flowed throughout her body and centered on her pussy and nipples.

"Good. Now, I'm going to pull out the rabbit flogger and do a little flogging."

"Yes, Sir." Her breathing increased. She enjoyed the rabbit flogger. It wasn't sting-y, but a nice caress, although Logan could make it thud against her skin quite well.

The first swats were against her upper thighs, both inside and out, moving up over her abdomen, and around her breasts. Each swat made the little jewels sway, which in turn, made her nipples throb more and her pussy clench with need.

Her muscles relaxed, and her body accepted the light flogging easily. Ellie closed her eyes, enjoying Logan's caresses when he paused the flogging. Soothing her skin, only to start up again. Until now she hadn't realized how keyed up she'd been waiting for tonight.

While she'd enjoyed planning the Halloween party, she hadn't been sure how Max or any of the other Doms would react to what she and the other subs had done. But they'd all been good natured, and it went well.

"Still with me, Ellie?" Logan's breath was warm on her cheek.

"Yes, Sir." She let her thoughts go.

"Good." The flogger was put down, and Logan began running his hands over her body. Her arms first, then over her neck. He tapped the jewels making her squirm, before trailing a finger over her belly to her thong.

Her breath came out in a whoosh as his finger moved over her fabric-covered pussy. Not that there was much fabric there. He knelt between her legs. "You smell delicious."

"Is that a good thing, Sir?" She wasn't sure if she should be embarrassed that he could smell her or be happy he liked her scent.

"A very good thing." He slid his fingers to the elastic of her thong, then dove under the fabric to stroke her.

Ellie moaned as he toyed with her clit before slipping his finger into her pussy. "So wet and warm."

She wanted to thrust her hips to take his finger deeper, but she couldn't. The restraints were doing their job and increased her need. Gone was her vulnerability; now she wanted Logan and to find the bliss she always found in his arms.

"More, please, Sir."

"My pleasure." He moved her thong aside, and his lips covered her mound.

Her neck arched as he licked her. So sexy. She loved the way Logan took care of her. He never minded going down on her, actually seemed to enjoy it. Her eyes closed as he pushed two fingers into her pussy.

He teased her clit with his tongue while he finger-fucked her. She wasn't going to last long. Her body had already been on high alert from the flogging, and now her toes curled.

She opened her mouth, trying to draw more air into her lungs. Her muscles tightened around his fingers, but Logan didn't stop; he kept thrusting and licking her. If he didn't stop soon... He curled his fingers inside her and stroked that special spot.

She cried out as she climaxed, leaving her overwhelmed for a moment. She was trembling in the chair, but Logan coaxed her through her orgasm and kept caressing her until the tremors settled down.

She felt Logan move her thong back into place and trail wet kisses up her body to her breasts. He removed the first clamp and gently sucked the nipple. The slight pain made her moan. He moved to her other breast and repeated his actions, but this time, the slight pain shot straight to her clit. Her body was primed.

"Damn," she muttered as a small orgasm shook her body.

"I've got you sweetheart." Logan's soft voice kept her grounded and stopped her from floating away in a sea of pleasure.

He caressed her right arm as he released the restraint, lowering her arm to her lap before doing the same with her left. The leg restraints were next. Ellie breathed through her mouth, trying to process the sensations. She almost laughed. She was enjoying the aftermath of Logan's domination and her submission. A blanket was placed around her, then Logan lifted her into his arms.

Ellie laid her head against his shoulder, reveling in the feel of his strong arms around her. Logan was a man she could fall in love with. The thought flitted across her brain, and she pushed it aside. No deep thoughts tonight. She wanted to enjoy this bliss for a while longer.

* * * *

"Time warp," Sierra yelled.

Ellie glanced up from where she sat on the sofa with Logan. Her bra was back in place. Her eyes were sparkling with energy and pleasure.

"Go." He could tell she wanted to join the women.

It was after midnight, and most of the club had finished their scenes. All were waiting for the surprise in the garden.

Logan made his way to the bar, laughing as the subs danced, though he only had eyes for Ellie. She looked very relaxed out there with everyone, and it made Logan happy. He liked it when Ellie was enjoying herself.

When the song ended, another one took its place, but Ellie made her way to where he sat at the bar.

"That was fun," she said, breathless.

"I've never seen you dance like that."

"All right. It's almost one," Sierra announced.

Everyone moved toward the doors to the garden. The crowd had thinned a bit, but not much.

"Tonight, we have another special surprise in the garden," Sierra said.

"Excuse me, Sir. I need to get ready." Ellie slipped from his grasp and joined the other subs by Sierra's side. Sierra nodded, and they slipped through the garden door.

"What is going on?" Colby yelled.

"Colby, Sir, everything is fine." Sierra grinned. "Your subs are hiding in the garden for you to find. But I do have to warn you, there are surprises in the garden. Witches, vampires, and I do believe some werewolves."

A murmur went through the crowd. "If you catch your sub before you're caught by any supernatural creatures, then you win."

"And if we don't?" Gabriel asked.

"Then the Dominant will have to make a sacrifice of their sub's choosing," Sierra said. A knock sounded. "All right. You have forty-five minutes."

Sierra threw the door open.

Logan followed the group of men out.

"What the hell?" Max stopped in his tracks.

Logan almost started laughing. The women had not only decorated the garden hedges with spider webs and fake spiders, there were fairy lights hanging everywhere and the bushes were rustling.

"I'd hurry, gentlemen, before some of the creatures come hunting you."

Max grabbed Sierra by the waist. "I claim my prize," he announced.

Several men rushed into the maze. Logan waited a minute until the rush was done to start his search for Ellie. How hard could it be?

* * * *

"Five minutes," Sierra's voice came over the loud speaker.

Logan shook his head. He'd seen a few of the subs captured by their Doms, but many of the Doms had fallen to creatures of the night. Ellie had an advantage since she was in on the planning, but the other subs had also been in on the planning.

Turning a corner, Logan found himself at a dead end. The maze shouldn't be that hard, yet he couldn't find his Ellie. He froze. *His.* Yes, Ellie was his. With determination, he retraced his steps.

He heard laughter ahead. Was that Ellie? He wasn't sure. Another dead end. "Two minutes." Logan shook his head, starting back the way he came, and ran into a witch.

"Now I've got you, Sir." A rope was thrown around him, pinning his arms to his sides. "My prize."

Logan stared at Ellie. "How the heck…"

She tugged on the rope and walked him out of the maze, and the other men groaned.

"Another one bites the dust," Damon commented.

"Who's missing?" Sierra asked.

"Lara, Colby, Regina, and Dane."

"We're here. I've got my prize," Dane said, walking out with Regina in his arms.

"Time's up," Sierra yelled.

"Lara, come out," Colby called.

A giggle sounded behind Logan, and he turned to see Lara standing there, grinning like the Cheshire cat. How had she snuck up behind him?

"Lara," Colby yelled again.

"Make your way to the front, Colby," Sierra commented.

After a few minutes, Colby emerged, looking disheveled and a little upset. "Sierra, where is she?"

"I'm right here." Lara ran out from behind Logan and into Colby's arms.

"Minx." Colby lifted her into the air.

"And that concludes tonight's games," Sierra said. "There is still food and, of course, playtime if you want. I hope everyone enjoyed themselves tonight."

Ellie swept off her witch's hat and smiled at him. "Since I caught you, I win, Sir."

"How many of us did you catch tonight?" He noticed that most of the subs had dropped the sir or ma'am during the garden play.

"You, Zeke, Oliver, and Gabriel, and he wasn't too happy, Sir. And of course, Colby." Ellie put her arm through his after they walked back into the club.

"I bet. But since you won, what are your demands?"

Ellie stared at him. "Let me think…"

Someone squealed, and they turned to see Regina being trussed up on Frankenstein's lap. Logan shook his head. "I've been meaning to ask about Frankenstein."

"He's solid. Usually, he's used as a photo prop. One of my vendors takes it to Halloween parties, and people sit in his lap for pictures."

"I don't like the usually there."

Ellie laughed. "Yeah. In this case, we rigged Frankie with a removable dildo for people to sit on."

Logan's gaze went back to Regina. Yep, he could see her squirming on the dildo, Dane teasing her. "And I thought Doms were sneaky."

"Sometimes we subs have to be too."

Logan drew Ellie into his arms. "I'm your prize for tonight."

"Yes, you are." She leaned against him and tilted her head up. "Take me home to our bed. That's my demand."

"One I'm more than happy to fulfill."

Chapter 14

The two weeks following the Halloween party flew by. Ellie looked at her work calendar. There were parties lined up, a few in November and a lot more for December. This was her busy time of year.

Everyone wanted to throw a Christmas party. She never took on New Year's parties because they were, frankly, too much work. Her phone beeped, and she glanced at the text message.

Logan: *Hi sweetheart, dinner at my place tonight? Or do you want to go out?*

Ellie: *Your place sounds great. I'll pick up some groceries, and we can cook together.*

It was one of her favorite things to do with Logan when they had time. She smiled. She'd grown close to Logan faster than she ever thought possible. He'd found a way into her heart, and she didn't mind.

Logan: *Perfect. Grab everything we need to make pizza, and don't forget beer.*

Ellie laughed and sent him laughing emojis. Her business phone rang, and she picked it up.

* * * *

Logan grinned at Ellie's reply. The past two weeks had been busy for both of them, but they spent Saturday nights at the club at the very least. Each week, Logan found himself falling more and more for Ellie.

Part of him acknowledged it was too fast. They'd only known each other a couple of months, but another part of him knew she was the right woman for him. Did Ellie feel the same way?

He wasn't sure. She hadn't mentioned the hazards of his job for a while now. It was sensitive subject, and he rarely talked about it with her. Maybe it was better to keep his feelings to himself and see where things led.

They had fun in and outside of the club, and he enjoyed the day shift. It gave him more time to do things in the evening and on weekends. When he'd worked the twelve-hour shifts, four days on and three days off, he'd felt like he was always rushing to get things done. Now, he was able to do tasks every day and nothing piled up.

His radio went off. "Back-up needed at four-six-three Broad Street. DV in progress."

"LW seven twenty responding." Flipping on the sirens, Logan took off. Domestic violence calls were never fun. When he arrived, another unit was there, along with the first responding officers.

Logan and his fellow officers stood back while the responding officers knocked on the door. They waited. There was shouting from inside the house. Logan put his hand on his firearm and waited.

They knocked again. The door was thrown open, and a loud bang was heard. One of the responding officers flew backward as his partner drew his gun and fired. Logan rushed to the downed officer as a woman inside the home screamed.

"LW seven twenty, need two ambulances , officer down. Repeat officer down. Suspect down." Logan reached for the officer's neck. He had strong pulse. Logan looked at his chest and let out a breath.

They weren't required to wear bullet proof vests on the job, but many of them did, him included. "Bill, you okay?" Logan asked.

"That fucking hurts." Bill groaned.

Logan let out a breath. "Ambulance on the way. Just lie still." His heart was pounding as he looked up to see the other officers shaking their heads and a woman crying.

Paramedics pulled up and jumped out of their vehicles. One pair ran toward him, the other toward the house. Logan stepped back as they moved in to check on Bill.

Logan glanced at his watch. There was no way he was going to make it home by dinner tonight, not with the paperwork this call would require. He pulled out his phone and texted Ellie that he needed to cancel dinner, but he'd pick her up for the club tomorrow night. He was careful to tell her he'd be on paperwork from a call for a few hours so she didn't worry.

Ellie answered with a hugging emoji and told him she'd meet him at the club, since Sierra, Crystal, and Tessa were taking her out to dinner to thank her for the Halloween party. Logan gave her the thumbs up emoji.

* * * *

Logan made his way into Wicked Sanctuary Saturday night with a heavy heart. Bill, the friend who'd been shot in the vest yesterday, went into cardiac arrest shortly after and died.

Logan found Ellie sitting in the sub area with Sierra and Crystal. His mood lightened seeing her. He didn't want to play tonight, just hold her in his arms.

Ellie jumped up when she saw him. "Logan, what's wrong?"

He shook his head and held his hand out to her. Instantly, she placed her hand in his. "Ladies," he said as he led Ellie away and over to one of the quiet areas. He plopped down on the sofa and drew her onto his lap.

Ellie laid her head on his shoulder, one arm around his neck, the other on his chest. Logan closed his eyes and breathed in her fresh scent, and his muscles relaxed. He needed her in his arms, to feel her heartbeat, the warmth of her skin.

He wasn't sure how long they sat that way before her fingers traced his cheek. "What happened?" she asked softly.

Logan didn't want to tell her, but she deserved the truth. "An officer passed this afternoon."

"Oh, Logan." She pressed herself closer to him. "I'm so sorry. How old was he?"

"Thirty-five." Almost the same age he was—too damn young.

Ellie stiffened in his hold, and Logan didn't blame her. "He was young."

"Yes. He had a heart attack." He opened his eyes. "Ellie, I didn't want to tell you this, but I will because I believe in open and honest communication between us." She nodded, her eyes filled with concern. "He was shot in the line of duty yesterday."

A small gasp left her lips. "He was wearing his vest, but the blast hit him square in the chest. While the vest protected him, the impact of the bullet messed up his heart rhythm. The doctors did everything they could, but they couldn't stabilize him, and he died."

Tears filled her eyes, and Logan cupped her cheek. "I know you don't want to hear this."

She shook her head, and leaned her cheek into his palm. "You need to get this out. I didn't hear anything about a robbery or anything like that." Her voice was soft.

"It was a domestic violence call." He took a breath and let it out. "They can be unpredictable. I was one of the backup officers called in." He shivered. It could have easily been him. The realization sent a cold chill through him.

What if it had been him? Would he have done anything differently? He didn't think so, and second guessing the what ifs wasn't a path he wanted to follow.

"That's awful."

"It is."

"Does he have a family?"

"A wife, but no kids. They were trying."

"She must be devastated."

"I'm sure she is." He'd pay his respects tomorrow.

"I'm glad you told me."

Logan gazed down at Ellie. She seemed sad at the news, but not upset. She was calmer than he expected. "Do you mind if we just sit here and hold you?"

"I'm fine with that."

"Thank you." He brushed a kiss over her temple and closed his eyes again.

* * * *

Ellie fought to keep her breathing normal. An officer had been killed, and Logan was there when it happened. Her heart hurt for the officer's wife, and it cracked for Logan and for herself. She had to admit, she wanted want to jump out of his arms and run.

She couldn't.

197

The devastation on Logan's face as he told her what happened kept her in his arms. He needed comfort, and she'd give it to him, even if every instinct in her said run. She wanted to be with Logan. Hell, she loved him.

She stopped breathing for a moment. She loved Logan. But could that love withstand him dying on the job? She didn't know, but she needed time to think. While she wanted to be with Logan, her fear of losing him was stronger.

It would be like losing her brother all over again, but a thousand times worse. She wasn't sure she'd be able to withstand it. For right now, she'd lay quietly in his arms and let him recover.

As he held her, her mind kept going over everything he said. And each conclusion was worse than the one before. To protect herself, she needed to bow out of his life. This way he could solely focus on his job and not be distracted by her.

Her heart contracted, and she fought to breathe. It had to be done no matter how much it hurt. It was the only way to keep Logan safe. But she would never be the same.

* * * *

Logan walked into Ellie's kitchen the next morning. He'd slipped on his pants, but that was it. They'd sat for several hours in the club last night. He'd followed Ellie home, but his heart was heavy and his mind as well. Ellie refused to let him leave.

She tugged him into her apartment, helped him undress, and put him in her bed. He slept with her in his arms all night. This morning, he was feeling better.

"Good morning, sweetheart," he said, slipping his arms around her waist for a hug.

"Good morning." She grabbed a mug and filled it with coffee.

Logan released her to take the mug, but something was off. Ellie wasn't her normal bright self, and she barely reacted to his hug. "You okay?"

"Logan, I think…" Her voice trailed off. She cleared her throat. "I think we need some time apart."

Why wasn't he surprised by the request? Probably because he knew in his gut it was coming. It still hurt. He set the mug on the counter and turned her to face him. He could see her mind turning things over and over.

Heck, he couldn't blame her. Yesterday's events had shaken him as well. Maybe them being apart was a good idea, no matter how much it hurt. It would give her time to think things through.

"I understand." He took a deep breath.

"I'm sorry," she whispered.

He shook his head. "Take all the time you need, Ellie." He leaned down and brushed a kiss over her lips. "I'll wait for you."

She nodded.

Logan turned and walked into the bedroom, finished dressing, then quietly left. Ellie hadn't moved from her position in the kitchen. He wanted to go to her and tell her everything would be okay, but that wasn't a promise he could keep.

He unlocked his vehicle and climbed in. His heart cracked. It was better this way. They both needed time to sort out what had happened. While he'd rather they did it as a couple… He blew out a breath as he started his SUV.

It was going to be a couple of long weeks for the department, and they were all going to be on edge for a while. Maybe this was for the best. Time apart from Ellie would help him straighten out in his head what had happened as well as give her time.

Being apart from Ellie wasn't going to be easy. He loved her. Logan pulled to the curb. He loved Ellie. Why hadn't he realized that before? Now what was he going to do? He almost turned the SUV around to go back to her apartment.

No, she needed time, and he would give her that. It was the least he could do. But he wasn't going to wait too long before he went after her.

Chapter 15

Logan woke on Thanksgiving morning with a heavy heart. He missed Ellie. Giving her time was the hardest thing he'd ever done. He'd texted her a few times, but her answer was always the same. "I need time."

The department was still healing over Bill's death. All the investigations had concluded, showing there was nothing they could have done differently, and most breathed a sigh of relief.

He still wondered if there was something they could have done so Bill wouldn't have gotten shot. Logically, he knew they'd done everything by the book, but in his heart, he grieved.

Bill had been laid to rest two weeks ago, yet Logan couldn't chase away the feeling that something was amiss. He'd begged off invitations to Thanksgiving dinner. He'd taken a couple of days off, so he had a long weekend.

After breakfast, he planted himself on the sofa and turned on the football game. That was the ticket. He could lose himself in the games this weekend.

A little after noon, his phone rang; he sighed when he saw the name on the display. "Hi, Mom."

"Logan, sweetie. I'm so glad you answered."

His mother's soft voice soothed the bleeding wound in his heart. "I always answer you."

"I wanted to call and tell you Happy Thanksgiving. I wish you could have flown back East and celebrated with us."

"I'm sorry I couldn't. The weather is too unpredictable this time of year." Even though he had a long weekend, flying to the East Coast and back could be risky. Plus, he hated traveling around the holidays. And who wanted to be around someone in his mood anyhow?

"I understand. How are you doing? How's the job?"

"I'm good. The job is fine."

"Logan, what is going on?"

"I don't know what you mean, Mom."

"It's in your voice. Did something happen at work?"

Logan shook his head. His mother, even over three thousand miles away, could tell something was wrong. With a sigh, he told her the story about Bill and what happened.

"Oh honey, I'm so sorry. Don't let it affect you too much. Your father wouldn't want that."

Those words caught Logan's attention. "I don't understand, Mom. Dad's death devastated you."

"Oh honey, in the beginning, yes. It was a shock, but after a few months, I began to get on with my life."

"But you were always sad." So many times, he remembered his mother would sit and stare at his father's picture on the mantle.

"I was sad because your father wasn't there to see you kids growing up. He would have been so proud of what you've accomplished, heck, what all you kids have accomplished."

"How can you be so sure of that, Mom?"

"Because we talked about it all the time. He was proud of you going to the academy and following in his footsteps."

Logan had known that. While his father didn't say the words, it showed in his face how proud he was when Logan graduated the academy. "How is Susan doing?"

"No changing the subject, young man." His mother chided. "Besides I want to know when you're going to find a nice young lady and settle down."

"I thought I had." The words slipped out before he could stop them.

"Tell me."

He found himself talking to his mother about Ellie, how she was a party planner and they met at Sierra's bachelorette party. He didn't tell her it was at a strip club but talked about how they hit it off and started dating. His mother had no idea about the club, and he planned on keeping it that way. He told her about Ellie's brother. "You see, when Bill died, for Ellie, it was like her brother dying all over again. I can't do that to Ellie. I can't hurt her that way." The words tumbled from his lips. Was that why he was giving Ellie time? He was afraid of making her a widow? He froze. He was thinking about Ellie being his wife? Damn straight he was.

"I see. Have you thought about how you would feel if something happened to Ellie?"

His heart clenched. "That's different, Mom."

"Is it? You told me about some crazed client. That could happen again."

"The odds are astronomical with Ellie."

"And while you being killed in the line of duty is higher, it's not worth giving up."

He shook his head. "Mom…"

"Hush, young man. Yes, I was hurt when your father died, but we had years together. I had you, your brother, and your sister to take care of yet. You had just graduated from the academy, but your brother was just eighteen and Susan fifteen. Each day, watching you all grow up was my blessing and got me through. I'm not going to say I didn't worry about you being on the force, but I was so proud. And I would never have stopped you from joining. You were meant to be a police officer, son."

Logan let her words sink in.

"Don't let fear of what might happen stop you from committing to this young lady."

"I'll think about it. But it isn't all my fear." This wasn't just about him. Logan was no longer sure Ellie could accept his job long term.

"You can work this out with her. Now, am I allowed to visit at Christmas? I'd like to meet your Ellie."

He chuckled. "I'll take some vacation so we can spend time together." Though he couldn't vouch for Ellie. Logan put a fist over his heart. Damn, he missed her.

He heard his sister's voice in the background.

"I need to go. I love you, Logan. Listen to your heart."

"Love you, too, Mom." The line went dead. Logan sat back on the sofa. He had some thinking to do.

* * * *

Ellie flopped down on her sofa Friday night. Thank goodness the Thanksgiving holiday was over, but now they were in full-fledged Christmas mode, and everything reminded her of what she'd lost. Lord, she was tired. Since her breakup with Logan, she'd been working ten to twelve hour days. She even brought her two temp employees on as full-time employees.

Had she bitten off more than she could chew? Probably. She hadn't turned down a job, because keeping busy didn't allow her to think about Logan. She huffed. Like he was far from her thoughts.

Nothing had helped. She missed Logan so bad she ached all over. Heart and soul, wasn't that the saying? Was he all right? Had he found peace with the death of his friend?

The downstairs intercom rang. Who could be here? Rising from the sofa, she walked to the door and pushed the intercom button. "Yes."

"Hey, Ellie, open up."

Ellie heard the smile in Sierra's voice and pressed the button. She opened her front door and within a few minutes, Sierra and Tessa were coming down the hall, arms loaded.

"What is all this?" Ellie asked.

"Intervention time," Sierra said, sweeping past her into the apartment.

"What?" Ellie could only stare at the two women as they moved into her kitchen. Pizza boxes landed on the counter, and Tessa unloaded the two bags she carried.

"Pizza, beer, or wine. Pick your poison, because it's time for you, Miss Ellie, to talk with us," Tessa said.

Ellie closed her front door. "I'm fine."

"Sorry girl, not buying it. You look like crap," Sierra said.

"You've lost weight, and you're not coming to the club, so we decided to stage this intervention," Tessa commented, pulling out paper plates and napkins. "If you don't pick a drink, I'll pick for you."

"Beer, then. Geesh." While happy to see her friends, Ellie wasn't ready for any sort of girl talk. Hell, she hadn't even sorted out her own thoughts. How could she talk about her feelings if she didn't know what they were? All she felt was hollow. Like something was missing from her life.

Logan was missing.

"Besides, we brought dessert." Sierra pulled out a wrapped cake from another bag, bringing Ellie back into the here and now.

"Is that—" For the first time in a while, Ellie's stomach growled.

"Yes, it is. Carmel pecan fudge cake, compliments of Lara." Sierra set it on the counter. "But real food first."

"I don't know if I'd call pizza real food," Ellie commented, but she was happy to have friends who wanted to help her.

They piled their plates, and each took a bottle of beer and went into the living room.

"What happened with you and Logan?" Sierra asked once they'd eaten and were on their second beer.

"Sierra." Tessa waved her hands in the air. "Have some tact, woman."

"I have none. I've been around Max too long."

Ellie grimaced. "We broke up."

"Why?" Sierra asked.

"Never give this woman beer," Tessa said. "She has no filter."

"It's okay." Ellie sat back in her chair and took a deep breath. "A few weeks ago, Logan and I met at the club, and when he came in that night, I knew something was wrong."

"That was the night you two sat over in the quiet corner, then left early?" Tessa commented.

Ellie nodded. "You've probably heard about the officer killed." They both nodded. Ellie took a deep breath and told them what happened.

"You're worried Logan will be killed on the job," Sierra said.

"Yes. It would be worse than when my brother died." Her heart squeezed. It would be a thousand times worse. She loved Logan. No matter how hard she tried to bury it, to deny it, that love was still there in her heart.

"Ellie," Sierra started and then hiccupped.

"Good thing I drove," Tessa said.

"I'm not drunk," Sierra protested. "Ellie, you have to understand that the chance of Logan dying on duty might be greater than any of us dying in an accident, but I bet it's not that much bigger."

"But he puts himself in danger every day." Ellie understood Logan's job was dangerous and accidents happened.

"Does he?" Tessa asked.

Ellie opened her mouth, then shut it.

"That got you thinking, didn't it?" Tessa looked proud of herself.

"You know, you were upset after the incident when he was knocked over," Sierra said. "But you handled it well."

"On the outside maybe, but on the inside, I was dying."

"That makes you human." Sierra waved her hands. "It's okay to be scared, but don't let it control your life."

Ellie shook her head. "I've felt for a long time that commitment wasn't for me. My parents divorced and have remarried other people too many times to count."

"That analogy is bullshit," Tessa said.

"Who's got the potty mouth now?" Sierra quipped.

"Just because your parents couldn't commit doesn't mean you can't. My parents are divorced. Best thing that ever happened to them and, eventually, for me," Tessa told her.

"Damon's and Max's jobs aren't dangerous," Ellie said.

"No, but there's nothing to say that Max couldn't be in a car accident that could kill him."

"Or Damon could be hurt in a robbery at his store." Tessa laid her hand on Ellie's arm. "What we're trying to say is there are no guarantees in life. I refuse to let fear stop me from living my life to the fullest."

"I wish I was that strong," Ellie said.

"Ellie, don't you realize how strong you are?" Sierra asked.

"What?"

"Ellie, I've watched you. Hell, we've all watched you. You planned my wedding and my bachelorette party, and you took on that line of Doms like they were koala bears. They didn't scare you."

Ellie grinned. It felt good to smile. "They were a little intimidating."

Tessa and Sierra laughed.

"But," Sierra continued. "You didn't take any crap from them. Then you joined Wicked Sanctuary. We all watched you with Logan. You might have been nervous and a little anxious, but you played. You took a chance on a relationship with Logan."

"I thought I could handle it."

"And you did," Tessa said. "Don't let your brother's death mar what you have with Logan. It was tragic, yes. But he wasn't even on duty."

Damn it, they were right. Her brother's death at the convenience store had been a case of wrong time, wrong place. She had to wonder if her brother even thought about what he was doing when he confronted the robber? Probably not, Tommy had always felt he was invincible.

But Logan never acted that way. Plus, he hadn't kept anything from her regarding his job. He was open and honest.

Ellie sat up in her chair. "What have I been thinking?"

"Don't borrow trouble is a phrase I've always liked," Sierra said.

"I agree," Tessa commented.

Ellie sat there in silence for a few minutes. Why hadn't she seen that? Her brother wasn't killed on duty. Yes, Logan had been hurt once, but that had been more accidental than anything. The second time, he was just at the scene, nowhere in the middle of it.

Logan also told her he didn't take chances, that he was well aware of how dangerous his job could be. He even mentioned he wore a bullet proof vest even when other officers didn't. He was doing everything he could to be safe.

And what about her? Her job wasn't dangerous, but she'd had to deal with disgruntled partners when the divorcing spouse wanted a divorce party. She'd never let that stop her.

"The lights are coming on."

She put her face in her hand. "What have I done? And how can I fix it? What do I do now?"

"We can help with that," Tessa said.

Chapter 16

Monday morning, after chatting with Sierra and Tessa Friday night, Ellie had a plan. She'd just put her purse in her desk when the bell on her front door jingled. Ellie smoothed her hands down her pants and walked out.

Her breath caught in her throat when she saw two uniformed officers standing there.

"Ms. Tanner, I'm Sergeant Jenson. I'm not sure you remember me."

"I do, Sergeant." They'd met the day Logan was taken to the hospital for the bump on his head. Her heart pounded. "Is it Logan?"

He nodded, and Ellie's legs almost gave out. She reached out and caught a hold of a chair. Her breath shuddered in and out of her lungs. "Is he…" She couldn't say the word.

"No, ma'am. He's on his way to Pleasant Valley General."

"Let me get my purse." Ellie was back in seconds. "Let's go." She needed to get to Logan. She had to see him. To tell him she was sorry for the way she acted, and how much she loved him. Even if this was their last conversation.

No! She wouldn't think that way. Logan was strong and healthy.

"We'll drive you," the Sergeant said.

"Fine. Let's get there." Ellie climbed in their unmarked car, and they were off. En route, Ellie texted Sierra, telling her she was on the way to the hospital, and Logan had been hurt.

That was all she knew. Within seconds, Sierra responded, telling her to believe in love, and her friends would be there shortly. Ellie put her phone away. "Can you tell me what happened, Sergeant?"

"I don't have the full story yet. There were on a call, and shots were fired. We had three officers rushed to the hospital."

He'll be all right. Ellie kept telling herself. They were pulling up to the emergency entrance in record time. She tossed a thank you over her shoulder to the officers as she raced inside.

The nurse at the desk nodded and pressed the button so she could get inside the ER. Doctors and nurses rushed everywhere. Ellie glanced left, then right. By then, the sergeant caught up to her.

"We've been given use of the large lounge due to the number of people," he said, pointing in the right direction.

Ellie saw what he meant when they walked in. There were seven officers and various family members of the other officers who'd been hurt. The grief in the room hurt Ellie's heart, and panic tried to take hold. *Be strong.* She would keep her faith in Logan. She had no choice. She loved him beyond anything she'd ever known before. He would live. He had to.

She found a spot near the door she knew the ER docs would come through, stood, and prayed, begging them to keep him alive.

"You must be Ellie, Logan's girlfriend," a young officer said, walking up to her.

"Yes." Logan called her *his girlfriend*.

"I'm Nate, Logan's partner." He held out his hand. Ellie took it. "I'm sorry we're meeting under these circumstances."

"Me too." Ellie swallowed. "What happened?"

"It was a bit crazy," he said.

Ellie glanced behind her at the door—not the one she wanted to see someone come through— as someone walked in. Not just one person but eight. Max, Sierra, Crystal, Jordan, Damon, Tessa, Sage, and Brady. They all rushed over to her as Nate backed away.

"Ellie." Sierra gathered her into her arms as the other women surrounded them. The men provided a protective barrier for the women.

"I'm okay," Ellie said.

"I'll see if I can find out what is going on?" Brady said.

Ellie looked at Sage. "Brady's a doctor. If anyone can get information out of the nurses, it's him," Sage said.

"It's getting crowded in here, I'm going to see if we can use the other room," Max said and he left.

"I can't believe you're all here." Her friends had come to give her support. She glanced at Sage.

"Don't give me that look, girl," Sage said. "You're one of us, and I will always support anyone from the club. Besides, I like you."

"High praise coming from her," Damon commented and was rewarded with one Sage's glares.

Max returned and talked with Sergeant Jenson before joining them. "I've gotten permission to use the other waiting room so we're not so crowded in here. I've also told Jenson if any other family members want to join us, they're welcome if they feel this room is too crowded."

Ellie nodded, though she was hesitant to leave this door.

"If the doctor doesn't find us, Brady will," Max said, nudging her toward the other waiting room. "I promise."

Nodding, she and the group trooped to the waiting room Ellie remembered from the first time she was here. That seemed so long ago now. A few minutes later, another woman and her family, along with Nate and another officer joined them. Ellie should go talk to them, but she couldn't. Her brain and heart were frozen in time. All she could do was wait to hear and pray that Logan made it through.

Ellie paced, unable to be still for even one moment or she'd start to cry and never stop. She needed to know what had happened. When Brady walked into the room, his face was grim. Ellie grabbed Sierra's hand.

"All three officers are in surgery. They wouldn't give me much more than that. Everything was still pretty chaotic."

Surgery? Was it serious? Ellie couldn't breathe.

"Sit. Head between legs." She was pushed onto a chair and her head forced down. "Breathe, Ellie."

"Ellie." Someone squatted in front of her, holding her arms, rubbing them up and down, comforting. "Do not expect the worst. Logan is strong, and he has you to live for," Max said.

"I know," she whispered. "But what if…"

Max squeezed her arms, gentle pressure, grounding her. "There is no what if. You have to believe in him and your love for each other."

Ellie brought her head up. "How do you know Logan loves me?"

He smiled. "It's obvious to us. We've all been there." Max waved his hand at the others standing around her. "You both may not have admitted it yet, but we see it."

Ellie's eyes filled with tears. "You are the best adopted family a woman could have."

"I can't ask Logan's permission at the moment, but screw the rules," Max muttered, pulling her into his arms. "Just hold on to us, Ellie, and we'll get you through this."

* * * *

Two hours passed at a snail's pace. Damon ran out and got everyone food and coffee, but Ellie couldn't eat. She did drink some water. The other women refused food as well, but everyone thanked Damon.

Finally, a doctor walked in. He looked startled at all the people in the room. "I'm looking for Mrs. Adams."

The other woman stood up, and without thought, Ellie moved toward her. Mrs. Adams glanced at Ellie and then held her hand out. Ellie clutched it tight, almost afraid to breathe.

"I'm sorry, Mrs. Adams." That was all the doctor got out before Mrs. Adams screamed. Ellie didn't even think. She pulled the woman into her arms.

Oh, God. Oh, God. My worst nightmare is happening.

"I'm so sorry," Ellie said over and over again, so hurt for this woman she didn't know. So scared for herself. They clung to each other, both mired in the same hell.

Others in Mrs. Adams' family gathered close, and Ellie relinquished her hold and stepped back. She couldn't move, couldn't think. The ringing in her ears overwhelmed everything, and she clutched her head, trying to get it to stop.

Brady quietly conferred with the doctor. She should join him, demand answers, but Ellie couldn't move. Her heart broke for the other woman, for herself.

Please, Logan. Please live. You have to. I need you to know how desperately I love you. I can't live without you. Please, please, please. Live.

Another cry was heard down the hall. Ellie closed her eyes and sank down onto the chair. Logan had to be okay. He loved her. She loved him. He was careful; he told her that. He always wore his vest. She repeated those words over and over again.

Brady rejoined the group. "Nothing on Logan yet; he's still in surgery," Brady said softly.

The other family huddled in the corner, then they began to leave.

"Excuse me," a woman said.

Ellie looked up to find a young woman standing in front of her. She squatted and reached for Ellie's hands. "I wanted to thank you." She looked around. "To thank all of you, not only for the food but for the support."

"You're more than welcome," Damon said.

"We're taking Mom home to rest."

Ellie scrambled in her purse and pulled out her business card. "Please call me if you need anything. I'd—" Her voice broke. "I'd like to help and to be there."

Tears filled the young woman's eyes. "I hope your husband is okay." She gave Ellie a quick hug before leaving.

Husband. They assumed she and Logan were married. Ellie's eyes filled with tears. She hoped they had time to explore the idea of marriage.

Another doctor walked in. Ellie stood on wobbly legs as her friends surrounded her. Brady walked up to the doctor before he could speak. Max took one hand and Sierra the other. The doctor and Brady talked quietly, before the doctor came over to her.

"Mr. Wolfe is fine."

The only thing holding Ellie up as her legs gave out was Max and Sierra holding her. "He's okay?"

"Yes. He took a bullet to the leg. It nicked an artery, and once we were able to stop the bleeding, the bullet was removed. Pretty routine. Things were quite chaotic for a while with three officers being brought in."

Ellie took a breath.

"He'll be off his feet for a while. He's in recovery. You'll be able to see him shortly." The doctor left.

"Thank God," Nate muttered, and all eyes turned to him. His eyes were red. Ellie let go of Sierra and reached for his hand. "I'm so sorry for the loss of your friend."

He nodded, fresh tears filling his eyes. Sniffing them back, he spoke. "I'll go tell the boss. Ellie, if you need anything, call me." He handed a card to Jordan, then left the room.

"I need to sit," Ellie said. Max guided her to the chair.

"He's going to be okay," Max said.

"Yes." Her eyes filled with tears.

"The other officer?" She prayed he was alive.

"One other survived. One passed."

Ellie nodded. So the second cry she heard was joy and not pain. "How long before I can see Logan?"

"Probably about thirty minutes."

Ellie took a deep breath and closed her eyes. Thirty minutes to see the man she loved and tell him how much he meant to her. She could wait that long. Now that they had their whole lives ahead of them. She breathed. In and out. Grateful that everyone left her alone for these moments to collect her thoughts.

Thirty minutes. She'd see Logan in thirty minutes.

Chapter 17

Logan woke slowly, trying to figure out where he was. An annoying beep wouldn't let him sleep, damn it. He just wanted to drift away. Wait. Where was he? He opened one eye, then the other slowly. In a hospital? *Think, brain, think.* The last thing he remembered was showing up on the call and then shooting pain in his leg. Logan looked down, relieved to find his leg bandaged, but whole.

Thank God. But what about the others. He closed his eyes, playing back the call. Suspect armed, backup needed, then more shots fired after he went down. Other officers falling? How many hurt? Were any killed? Had it been an ambush? He didn't think so.

Instinctively, he reached out for Ellie. She wasn't there. Ellie. He sighed. He didn't want to tell her how much he loved her over the phone, and he doubted very much she'd want to come to the hospital to see him. Sensing movement in the doorway, he turned his head.

Was he hallucinating? Ellie walked in, her gaze on him. "Logan," she whispered as she rushed to his side and grasped his hand.

"You're here." The warmth of her skin against his told him he was fully awake and not hallucinating.

"Where else would I be, silly?" She ran her fingers through his hair and kissed his forehead.

Logan could only stare at her. She was so beautiful. "Ellie, I need to know. The other officers."

Her gaze skittered away from his, and she stayed silent. A death, at least one, he figured. How many officers had gone down? Two that he remembered. The pain everyone must be feeling, but especially his Ellie.

"I'm so sorry, Ellie."

"For what?" She snagged the chair with her foot, brought it close, and sat down, but never released his hand.

"For everything."

She shook her head. "I love you."

Logan blinked. "What?" Had he heard her right?

"I love you." Her voice was strong this time.

His heart pounded. "Oh, my Ellie. I love you so much." He reached for her, but the IV tubing wasn't long enough.

Her fingers trailed down his cheek. "We can embrace later. How do you feel?"

"Like I've been shot."

"Please don't joke."

"I'm sorry." He wanted to comfort her, but with the damn IV, he'd have to wait. "I'd like to talk with the doctor." He needed to know exactly what happened and what the prognosis was.

"I'll go get him." She stood.

"No." Logan tightened his hold on her. "Don't leave. Please. Just press the button for the nurse."

Ellie did as he said, and a nurse joined them in moments. "You're awake. That's good." She bustled over to the bed.

"I'd like to talk to the doctor."

"Of course, let me get your blood pressure right quick." The nurse glanced at Ellie.

"Logan, she needs your arm."

He squeezed her hand and released it. Ellie moved while the nurse took his blood pressure, then a temperature check and wrote down the numbers from the overhead monitor Logan was attached to. His patience was stretched thin by the time she finished. He wanted Ellie next to him and to talk with the doctor.

"All good. I'll go get the surgeon." The nurse left.

"Finally," he muttered.

"Behave yourself," Ellie said.

"Come back over here."

She shook her head. "Let the doctor come in first."

"It could be a while, and I want to touch you."

"I want that, too, but…" She shook her head.

Logan opened his mouth to argue, but closed it. She was right, the doctor would probably want to examine him. It didn't mean he liked it.

Several minutes later, the doctor walked in. "Mr. Wolfe," he said, then looked at Ellie.

"Ellie Tanner," she said, holding out her hand.

"My fiancée," Logan added.

The doctor nodded, then took some time to examine Logan, checking feeling in his leg and feeling something on top of his foot.

Logan didn't get a good look, but what he saw, he didn't much like. He tried to remember he still had his leg. That was the important part.

The doctor went over the procedure and treatment plan, and Logan was relieved when the doctor said his leg would heal up normally.

"Will I be able to return to duty?" Out of the corner of his eye, he saw Ellie stiffen.

"I don't see why not, as long as there isn't lasting damage, and I don't see anything at this point. Is there anything else?"

Logan shook his head, and the doctor looked at Ellie. "Thank you for saving his life," she said.

The doctor smiled and nodded, then left the room.

"Come here." Logan held his hand out.

"Bossy," she muttered but pulled the chair next to the bed and placed her hand in his.

Logan took her hand and raised it to his lips. "I'm glad you're here."

"I wouldn't be anywhere else."

He started to grin, but yawned instead.

"Rest," she said. "We have time."

Logan wanted to argue with her, but his eyes were already closing. "Stay," he whispered.

"I'm not going anywhere, my love."

My love. Those two words warmed his heart as he fell asleep.

* * * *

Logan opened his eyes. The chair where Ellie had been sitting was empty. "Ellie," he yelled. She couldn't have left him. He couldn't take it.

"Easy, Logan." Her voice came from across the room. "I was just in the bathroom."

"Come here." His voice was rough and dry, but he didn't care. He needed her close.

"Settle down." She retook her seat and held a straw to his lips. He drank, the cool water soothing his throat.

"Thank you."

"There is no need to get riled up."

"I was afraid you'd left."

"Not happening." She smiled. "I think you're stuck with me."

"That's good." His fingers tangled with hers. "I love you, Ellie." He wanted to tell her again.

"So you've said. I love you too."

Logan groaned, and Ellie reached for the call button. "I'll get the nurse."

"No. I'm fine." He squeezed her fingers. "I want to pull you into my arms and kiss you silly, but I really can't."

Ellie chuckled, and Logan glared at her.

"Take it easy, mister big bad Dom." Her voice was soft. "We'll have plenty of time to kiss when you come home."

"When did you figure out you loved me?" He had been surprised when she said those words the first time. Now that she said them again, he needed to know.

"A while ago, even though I never really admitted it to myself. But after a heart-to-heart talk with Tessa and Sierra, I knew just how much I loved you and didn't want to let you go."

"I think I've loved you since you stood in the strip club glaring at all of us. My defiant Ellie."

"I don't think I've ever been defiant, maybe a little rebellious." She leaned over and brushed a kiss across his cheek. "I'm sorry I panicked about your job and everything that went with it."

"You had every right."

"Maybe. I'm working on calming my worry about losing you due to your job. You're not like my brother, who thought he was invincible. I would like, at some point, to maybe talk to your mother about it."

"I think that would be a great idea. And you know I try to be careful. This was unavoidable."

"Tell me what happened?"

"A group of us responded to shots fired on the southeast side of town."

"Rougher side."

"Yes, it's not unusual, but we rarely find any issues."

"Today was different."

"Yeah." He shifted on the mattress and hit the pain pump button. "Three units got there before us. We exited our vehicles to see what was going on, and bam. Guns went off. I went down, and that was it. I think Nate dragged my ass behind the car, and I heard him call for help."

"An ambush?"

He shook his head. "I don't think so. I won't know for sure until the other officers report, and an investigation is done." Logan's face grew sober. "The other officers?"

"A total of three of you were hurt." She squeezed his hand. "One died."

"Who?"

"The last name was Adams."

"Bruce Adams, he's been on the force for almost thirty years."

Ellie closed her eyes. "His wife and I were together when the news came. I never want to hear someone scream like that again, but I know it can happen." Her voice caught.

"I'm so sorry you had to hear that, Ellie." He wanted to pull her into his arms and comfort her. Damn IV. "I want to promise that you'll never hear someone scream like that again, but I can't."

"I know." While there were tears in her eyes, her features were relaxed. "You're a great police officer and love your job. I'm not going to ask you to give it up. I'll learn to cope."

"You will?"

"I will; you'll see. I told you I love you. That means I love all of you, even if your job does scare me. I know you're careful."

"It doesn't look like that now," he commented.

Ellie shook her head. "You said you climbed out of your car and then shots rang out. I'm sure your first instinct was to dive for cover, but they were faster. I'm not going to say I'm not going to worry, but I'm not going to borrow trouble that I can't see or predict."

"I don't either." He took a deep breath. "I never wanted a lasting relationship until you."

"Why not?"

"My father was killed in the line of duty, and I always worried about leaving my partner alone."

"Oh, Logan."

"I had a long talk with my mother, and she told me love was worth the risk. You're worth the risk."

"You are too."

"As my fiancée, when I get out of here, you are moving in with me," he said.

"Yeah, you did call me that." Ellie laughed. "Damn right I am. You're going to need someone to take care of you."

"I want you for more than that, Ellie."

"I know. One step at a time."

EPILOGUE

Ellie grinned as she walked into Wicked Sanctuary. Logan was seated at the bar, surrounded by people. This was the first time they'd come to the club since he'd been hurt. Not that they hadn't seen their friends.

There wasn't a day that went by that someone from the club didn't stop by Logan's house to check in on them. Heck, the first two weeks, everyone kept stopping by with food until Ellie begged them not to. The freezer was overflowing, and they had enough food to feed a small army. Now that Logan was mobile, he wanted to come to the club. It was time. They needed this time together.

The past six weeks hadn't been easy. His mother had fussed over him at Christmas and told Ellie she was ready for a daughter-in-law. She liked his mother, and the siblings they'd video chatted with.

Ellie also talked with Logan's mother, and she gave Ellie tips on being a police officer's wife. Ellie was grateful to have his mother to talk to.

Ellie walked up to the group. "Good evening, everyone."

Logan grasped her around the waist and pulled her to him. "About time you got here," he whispered in her ear.

"Sorry, Sir. I was catching up with the subs."

"What could you catch up on? They're always at the house."

"They're part of our family."

"Damn right," Max said.

Laughter rang out.

"Now this sounds like a party," a male voice said.

"Rafe." Max held out his hand. "It's great to see you."

"Thanks, Max. I'm finally back from a very long training course." Ellie smiled at Rafe when he looked at her. "And it looks like the new sub I've been hearing about is taken."

"You bet your ass. Look elsewhere," Logan said.

"Behave, Sir." Ellie grinned.

"Another one bites the dust," Damon said.

A cheer went up, and Logan nuzzled her neck.

"I love you so much," he whispered.

"Right back at you. I couldn't be happier."

"Good, because I got the all clear from the doctor. Tonight, you're mine."

"I've always been yours." Their lips met in a soft kiss. This was forever, and no matter what they would face in the future, they would face it together.

* * * *

Thank you for reading *Unmasked*, the eighth book in the Wicked Sanctuary series. If you enjoyed this book, please consider leaving a review on Goodreads, or your favorite retailer, and know that it would be greatly appreciated.

For new release information and news about Marie Tuhart, please join her newsletter.

If you enjoyed *Unmasked, Too Hot* will be released in May of 2024. You can pre-order now.

ABOUT THE AUTHOR

Marie Tuhart lives in the beautiful Pacific Northwest. She loves to read and write, and when she's not writing, she spends time with her two dogs, Tommy and Trina, family, traveling and enjoying life.

Marie is a multi-published author with The Wild Rose Press and Trifecta Publishing, and is self-published. To be alerted to her new releases, you can join Marie's newsletter or check out her website: www.mairetuhart.com

And for up-to-date information about releases, please consider joining Marie's mailing list.

OTHER BOOKS BY MARIE TUHART

Claimed by the Sheikh

Billionaire's Cowboy's Conquest

Tempt (Wicked Sanctuary Series)

Entice (Wicked Sanctuary Series)

Seduce (Wicked Sanctuary Series)

Ravish (Wicked Sanctuary Series)

Possess (Wicked Sanctuary Series)

Tantalize (Wicked Sanctuary Series)

Edged (Wicked Sanctuary Series)

Unmasked (Wicked Sanctuary Series)

Too Hot (Wicked Sanctuary Series) May 2024

Wicked Sanctuary Novella's:

Untamed

Power Play

Claiming Rose

PREVIEW OF *TOO HOT*

Brianna Copeland clapped to get her students' attention. "All right, everyone. Our special guests will be here shortly, so put away your books and take your places at your tables."

Her kids scrambled up from their places on the floor where they'd been reading and put their books away in the bins in the back of the classroom. Slowly, they took their seats at their tables. She smiled at them before glancing out the window.

A police car had pulled up a moment ago, and now a firetruck was arriving. Her students were so excited to be hearing from a real police officer and firefighter today. Her gaze was captured by the firefighter.

Oh my goodness. His dark blue shirt was stretched over broad shoulders and tucked into blue slacks. Her gaze continued down to a pair of black boots. Heat filled her body. She forced her gaze away from his feet in time to see muscular arms flex as he shut the fire truck door.

He turned his head, and Brianna started to look away but noticed he was calling out to the police officer who'd exited his vehicle. What were their names? Oh, yeah, Officer Wolfe and Firefighter Lyons.

Wolfe and Lyons, what a combination. She continued to watch as he shook hands with Officer Wolfe, and she shivered. How would it feel to have those masculine hands on her body? On her skin?

Brianna shook her head. What was wrong with her? She wasn't one to ogle men. But she kept watching until the two men disappeared.

"Miss Brianna," one of her students called.

She turned away from the window to see all her students at their desks. "Yes, Penny."

"How long before the fireman and policeman get here?" Penny wiggled in her seat.

"Shortly." She moved away from the window and smiled at her students. "Remember, fireman and policeman are not used much anymore because there are women in those professions now. Today, we use firefighter and police officer.

"Yes, Miss Brianna," the kids chorused.

"I'm going to be a firefighter," Winter said.

"Me, I'm going to be a cop," Cooper commented.

"You can be anything you want," Brianna said.

More voices joined in what they wanted to be when they grew up, and Brianna shook her head. They'd change their minds over the course of their lives, just as she had. She noticed movement at the classroom door and went to admit the visitors.

"I believe they're here," she said as the door opened to reveal the principal.

* * * *

"Hey, Rafe."

Rafe Lyons turned. "Logan." He walked over and held out his hand. "How are you doing? Feeling better?" Logan had been shot several months ago.

"Right as rain. I see your captain roped you into presenting at the school."

"Yeah, probably because I do double duty." The Pleasant Valley Fire Department wasn't big enough to require a full-time arson inspector, so he was a firefighter first, then an inspector.

"I get that. My boss offered to have others from the department come, but since it's second graders, they wanted to keep it basic."

"Makes sense." They walked toward the entrance. Out of the corner of his eye, Rafe saw a young woman standing at a window. Probably the teacher, but she looked too young. He let out a sigh. He was only thirty-five but felt older.

"I heard about the fire over on 20th Street. Anyone hurt?" Logan asked.

"No." Rafe ran his hand over his hair. "It's the third fire we've had in a week."

"Arson?"

"Not sure. There are no obvious clues." At the door, Rafe pushed the button, and within a minute, an older woman pushed it open. "Welcome, gentleman. I'm principal Meyers."

"Principal Meyers," Rafe inclined his head and held the door open. He disliked how schools had to be so locked up to keep the kids safe. Kids should be free to play. But it was the world they lived in.

Pleasant Valley wasn't a hot bed of shootings or anything that would threaten the kids, but he was glad they were taking precautions.

"Ms. Copeland's classroom is this way. The second graders are excited." She bustled her way down the hall with him and Logan following.

When she stopped in front of a door, Rafe grinned. The door had been decorated for them. Fire trucks, police cars, badges, ladders, hoses, and handcuffs. Kids this age had big imaginations. He reached for the knob and held it open for the principal.

The chattering of children reached his ears. The room went silent as the principal walked in, and Logan followed, then he closed the door behind him.

The principal introduced them. "Officer Wolfe and Firefighter Lyons, this is Brianna Copeland, the second-grade teacher."

"Welcome, gentlemen." The woman he'd seen at the window stepped forward with her hand outstretched.

Rafe's gaze met hers as he took her hand in his. If he hadn't been looking at her as closely as he was right then, he would have missed the slight darkening of those hazel eyes as they touched. He didn't want to let go. Logan cleared his throat. Rafe released her hand, and she shook Logan's hand.

"We're so glad you're here today." Her voice was soft and soothing. Rafe could see himself coming home at night and being able to relax with her.

What was wrong with him? He wasn't looking for a long-term relationship, but damned if his mind didn't go there with her.

"I'll head back to my office." The principal left the room.

"Would you like to stand or sit?" she asked.

Rafe kept his gaze on her. Her face was flushed. "I think standing will be fine."

"Yes." Logan nudged him in the side.

"Okay." She turned away.

"What's going on?" Logan whispered.

"Nothing." Rafe shook his head. A bomb of attraction had hit him the second their hands touched. Unusual for him and he wanted to pursue it.

"Well, keep it under wraps. We're in an elementary classroom."

Logan was right to remind him. He looked out at all the eager faces and counted quickly. Twelve kids. A good class size.

"All right. Please remember your manners. Raise your hand to ask a question, and wait to be called on," Ms. Copeland said to her class. She gestured to them. "The floor is yours." She moved to the back of the room.

"Hello, kids, I'm Officer Wolfe."

"And I'm Firefighter Lyons."

One of the little girls burst out laughing. "You're named after animals."

The class laughed, and Lyons and Wolfe chuckled.

"One might think that. So how about for today, you call us Rafe and Logan."

The kids turned to look at their teacher, and she nodded.

"Who has a question?" Logan asked. Twelve hands shot up, and off they went.

* * * *

Brianna leaned against the wall trying not to ogle the firefighter. Rafe. That was his name. She knew who Logan was since she was friends with Ellie, his girlfriend. Brianna hadn't met Rafe yet, but Ellie talked about him.

She listened as the men answered the kids' questions. They were patient and understanding.

"Miss Brianna, can we go out and look at the fire truck, please?" Cooper asked.

She glanced at the two men who were leaning against her desk at the front of her classroom.

"We don't mind," Logan said.

It was only eleven, and lunch wasn't until twelve. "Okay." The kids cheered. "Line up and no running." The kids jumped up and formed a line, starting at the door.

"Impressive," Rafe said when she grabbed her keys off the desk.

"You just have to know how to handle them." Brianna almost clamped her hand over her mouth. That came out all wrong. Rafe grinned. She shook her head and opened the door. She waited to close the door until Rafe and Logan were out of the room, then followed them outside.

Brianna was proud of her kids. They walked calmly and quietly outside and waited until Logan and Rafe could lead them to the vehicles. She hung back, allowing the kids to enjoy themselves.

Almost an hour later, the kids were out of questions and had been all over both vehicles. A bell went off.

"Lunch time," Penny yelled.

"What do you tell Officer Wolfe and Firefighter Lyons?" Brianna said.

"Thank you." Twelve pairs of eyes turned to her. "Let's go back to the classroom and then it will be time for lunch."

The kids ran for the door. Ellie, Logan, and Rafe followed after them.

"I believe you're friends with Ellie," Logan said after Ellie dismissed the kids for lunch.

"Yes. It's good to meet you." Brianna had met Ellie two months earlier when she was setting up a birthday party for one of the other teachers, and they'd become friends. "All healed up now?"

"I am. Is there anybody in this town who doesn't know I got shot."

Rafe clapped Logan on the shoulder. "No."

There was friendship there. "Ellie told me about it. I had read in the newspaper about the shooting, but no names were mentioned."

"I'm glad she talked about it." Logan's radio went off. "Excuse me."

Brianna's tummy flipped. She was alone with Rafe. "Thank you for being so good with the kids, Firefighter Lyons." She didn't know what else to say.

"Rafe. And you're welcome. The kids are fun to be around."

She nodded. "I should go out and help supervise lunch."

"I understand."

Brianna escorted Rafe out of the building. She wanted to stay and chat with Rafe, but a part of her told her to run. Not that it mattered, she'd probably never see him again.

You can pre-order *Too Hot* now

9 781954 847095